Skip Shaughnessy

and

the Surprise Family Union

Skip's Action Series

Book 4

Marjorie Strebe

And let us not be wearing in well doing: for in due season we shall reap, if we faint not.

Galatians 6:9

Table of Contents

Chapter 1

A Change in Plans

His one-hour drive home had been anything but quiet.

Wearing dark glasses to protect his light-sensitive eyes from the glaring sunlight, off-duty police officer Skip Shaughnessy listened attentively as his young bride talked non-stop.

Their honeymoon had been everything but a honeymoon. A letter from Cassandra's uncle caused them to make a detour to his ranch. That quick detour turned into a three-day whirlwind of adventure and suspense.

But when they left on their honeymoon, Skip's nine year old sister deeply mourned the loss of her big brother.

She'd said to him, "Dad went to Heaven to live with Jesus, and now that you're married, you're going to move away to live with Cassandra. And you're all the daddy I have. I don't want you to go away!" Stephanie burst into fresh tears.

Needless to say, he did something he shouldn't have done. He took her with him.

With mysterious happenings at a nearby farm and people disappearing, Skip's investigation brought him face to face with Stephanie's kidnappers, and he still had rope burns because of it. But this morning he met a special lady named Stephanie Rose Thompson who was en route to see her brother – his dad – not knowing that he had gone home to be with the Lord.

So here he was on his way home three days after leaving for his honeymoon. Cassandra chattered nonstop in the front passenger's seat, and Stephanie excitedly talked to Aunt Rose in the back seat.

After he dropped off Stephanie and Aunt Rose with his mother, he intended to take his young bride to Yellowstone National Park to enjoy a *real* honeymoon.

With a sigh of relief, he spun his metallic-blue Buick into his mother's driveway, but before he even had time to cut the engine, Stephanie started yelling.

"We're home! We're home! Come on, Aunt Rose. Come meet our mom." Stephanie threw open the back door and raced around the car, yanking open Rose's car door.

Skip stepped from the car and strolled around to open Cassandra's door. The minute Cassandra joined him, he kissed her and took her hand. "Let's go introduce Mom and Aunt Rose. Then I'll haul in the luggage that stays here, and we'll take off for Yellowstone. Just you and me."

"I'd like that," said Cassandra.

Holding hands, Skip and Cassandra strolled up the walk to the front door and entered without knocking.

"Skip!" chorused his three youngest little sisters.

Sandy, Suzi, and Scooter ran to greet him, flinging their arms around him.

Skip hugged the girls and hoisted three-year-old Scooter into his arms. It was the first time that he could remember in a long time that his four little sisters didn't knock him down when he came through the door. But then, Stephanie didn't run to greet him because she'd been with him all weekend, except when she got kidnapped.

Skip glanced around the room. He saw Cassandra disappear into the kitchen. Aunt Rose was sitting on the sofa with Stephanie, looking at her drawings.

"Did you meet Aunt Rose?" Skip asked his mother.

"Indeed, I did. I look forward to having a chance to get to know her. Your dad always talked so highly of his sister. How was your honeymoon?" asked Erin.

"Uh ... Don't ask," said Skip.

Erin laughed. "That bad, huh?" She handed him an envelope. "This came in the mail for you while you were gone."

Setting down Scooter, he slowly took the envelope from her and glanced at the return address. It was from the court system. Skip peeled it open and pulled out a single sheet of paper, reading the brief letter.

Skip looked at his mom. "I've been released to return to duty, effective immediately."

"That must be why Captain Kramer called this morning."

Skip raised an eyebrow. "Captain Kramer called here looking for me? Oh, boy. That can't be good."

He immediately knew that his leave time had been cut short. Although he still had four days coming, he hoped that the police department didn't require him to sacrifice them all. He could use one more day to prepare himself mentally for his sudden return to work.

In addition, he still had to help Cassandra pack up and move in with his family. He and Cassandra had left town immediately following their wedding reception. So the only things she had with her were those that she'd packed in her suitcase and taken on their honeymoon. And now it looked like he might have to return to work sooner than he'd expected.

Reluctantly, he picked up the receiver and dialed the police station, praying for one more day off. Unfortunately, Captain Kramer didn't sound sympathetic. He sounded exhausted.

"I hate to do this to you, Skip, but we're really shorthanded right now. You've been cleared by both a psychiatrist and the court system to return to work after that deadly shootout in Kenton. So I need you back here tomorrow."

"Tomorrow."

"I'm sorry, Shaun. No one wants to cut your leave short, especially me. But we're really in a crunch. A flu epidemic swept through the department right after you left, and a lot of the guys are home sick. Greg flew out east for a family emergency. A couple days ago Johnny and Pete wrecked their patrol car on a high-speed pursuit and landed in the hospital."

"You're kidding! A high-speed pursuit through this peaceful little town? Are they okay?"

"Yeah. Fortunately neither of them were seriously injured, but they'll both be off the street for awhile. So the few officers left are pulling sixteen-hour days. Even the chief and I are putting in long hours of overtime."

"I got the message. I'll be in tomorrow." With a heavy sigh, Skip hung up the phone and looked at his mother. "Well, there went our honeymoon."

"I'm sorry, Skip."

"Cassandra and I haven't had any time alone, so I think we're going to take off and spend the day together. I'll be home in time to get ready for work in the morning."

Erin raised an eyebrow. "Do you intend to stay out all night?"

Skip shrugged. "I haven't decided, but whatever we do, we're going to do it together." With a heavy sigh, he plodded back out to his car to haul in their luggage.

Chapter 2

A Lethal Threat

With Stephanie back home and Aunt Rose visiting from out-of-town, Skip knew the house would be a bustle of activity, and no one would even miss them. So after he hauled in the luggage, he hustled Cassandra out the front door before she got sucked into all the activity.

"Skip, where are we going?" she asked, running to keep up with him. "I wanted to stay and visit with your mom and Aunt Rose."

With a firm hold on her hand, Skip hustled her back to the car. "Don't worry, Cassie. You'll have lots of time to visit. That's a promise."

"Not if we're going to Yellowstone. We'll be gone for four days."

Skip opened the car door for her and seated her before trotting around the car and climbing into the driver's seat. Starting the engine, he backed out of the driveway.

"Yeah, that's true." Skip sighed. "Unfortunately, my leave's been canceled. I have to work tomorrow."

"How can that be? You were on administrative leave."

"Until the court system cleared me to return to work. I just received notification that I've been cleared. It came quicker than I expected, but I can't say I'm surprised. It was a clear-cut case of self defense, and I guess the Grand Jury recognized that."

"So if we're not going to Yellowstone, where are we going?"

"I just wanted to spend some time with you, Cassandra. Just the two of us today. Are you okay with that?"

Cassandra smiled. "I'm more than okay with it."

Skip glanced at her and back at the road. "Now, I know you wanted to learn how to drive. Do you have a learner's permit?"

"No."

"Then let's swing by WYDOT and grab you a driver's manual. Then, if you like, I know this great little area with some dirt roads. It's outside of the city limits, and you can practice driving all you want before you even have your learner's permit."

"Skip, isn't that illegal?"

"Probably, but because it's out of the city limits, no police officer will give us a ticket out there. I know many parents who've taken their kids out there for driving lessons, and the police actually encourage it. Makes them safer drivers in town."

Cassandra's eyes got big. "So I can start today? Well, let's go!"

Their first stop was the Wyoming Department of Transportation. Parking the car, Skip and Cassandra ran in and grabbed a driver's booklet before they closed for the day. Then they headed for that great little area outside of town for Cassandra to get her first driving lesson behind the wheel.

Since Skip's Buick was a standard, he had to teach her how to get the car moving from a complete stop before she could even go anywhere. Cassandra stalled the car time and time again, and when she finally got it moving, it jerked badly.

As the sun dropped below the horizon and its light faded from view, Cassandra finally managed to shift the car into third gear, which was fast enough to get some practice steering. But it was nearly dark, and she'd had enough driving practice for one day.

"Now that I'm finally moving, how do I stop this thing?"

"Let up on the gas," said Skip. Sitting in the front passenger's seat, he helped his young bride downshift into first gear while she guided the car to a stop.

"It's so much easier to stop than it is to go," said Cassandra.

"Indeed, it is." Stepping from the car, Skip hustled around to the driver's door and swung it open, preparing to switch seats with Cassandra.

Bright headlights illuminated the dirt road where they were stopped, and a little car headed right toward them, practically blinding Skip.

Because they were outside the city limits driving around on the deserted dirt roads, there were no street lights or oncoming traffic, so Skip had removed his dark glasses. But when that car turned toward them, he slipped them back on. Regardless, he still blinked and turned away from the light, practically blinded by the high beams.

A little white Datsun screeched to a stop directly in front of their car. Cassandra slid from the car, curiously eyeing the Datsun. The car's headlights blinked off, drastically reducing their ability to see specific details in the dimness of twilight, and three young men scrambled from the vehicle, surrounding Skip and Cassandra with guns.

Still seeing spots, Skip strained to identify these lads. Two of the boys were no older than he, but the third was definitely younger.

"Hands where we can see them!" commanded the tall, dark-haired lad.

Cassandra caught her breath, but Skip didn't move. His hands were already in the open. A sudden movement could startle one of these boys into pulling the trigger.

"Get on the other side of the car away from the road. *Now.*"

The same boy gave the orders. This youth was the leader. The other two hadn't said a word.

Needing to protect Cassandra, Skip took her hand and stepped around to the other side of the car, but the other tall boy seized her arm and jerked her over to them.

"Hey, let her go," ordered Skip. He wanted to go for his gun, but it was secured in his ankle holster underneath his right trouser pant leg. There was no way that he could retrieve his gun before one of these boys pulled the trigger.

Skip started toward them, but jerked to a stop when the leader grasped Cassandra's other arm and pointed his gun directly at her.

"I don't think so. Now, on the ground, or we'll pump her full of lead."

Chapter 3

Trouble on the Horizon

Skip studied their faces. Despite how dark it was, his car headlights were on, illuminating them just enough for him to see their expressions. These boys didn't have the harshness in their eyes that he usually saw in more hardened criminals. That caused him to suspect that this was more likely a prank. But did he dare run the risk? Their guns were small and black and blended in well with the darkness, so he had to assume they were real. If only he could get to his gun.

With Cassandra between them, clutching her arms on either side, and their guns aimed right at her, the two older boys slowly backed toward their car, dragging her along.

Skip was not about to stand idly by while they forced her into their car. There was no telling what they would do to her. He would die to protect her.

Tears coursed down her cheeks. "Skip."

Skip's eyes darted from one lad to another as he slowly approached the two older boys. With a firm grip on Cassandra's arms, the boys backed toward their car.

"Stay back, *or we'll kill her,*" cried the leader, pointing his gun at Skip.

The other boy followed his lead while the youngest dashed to the white Datsun and scrambled into the back seat.

They threatened to kill Cassandra, yet they both pointed their guns at him. Their boldness seemed to dwindle with every step that Skip closed the gap.

Calculating the distance between him and the armed young men, Skip saw that they stood exactly halfway between him and their car. As Skip slowly neared them, these once brave lads continued a slow retreat toward their vehicle, dragging Cassandra with them.

"Let her go." Skip took another step toward them.

"Don't come any closer, or we'll shoot."

These guys threatened big, but as he neared them, they were backing down. He wondered if they held toy guns, although it was too dark for him to tell. But it wasn't too dark to see that these guys were dragging Cassandra toward their car. Another couple of feet and they'd be close enough to shove her in and take off with her. And Skip couldn't let that happen. He had to act, *and he had to act now.*

With a quick two-step, Skip shuffled in. He snatched the gun from the leader and threw a punch at him.

The boy ducked and scrambled into the front passenger's seat of the Datsun.

Cassandra ran into Skip's arms as the driver's door slammed and the little white car screeched off. It was too dark to get the license plate number, and the car moved too fast.

Sitting in the back seat, Robby stared out the rear window at the couple they'd left standing on the dirt road, but they quickly faded from view. He turned back around to look at his older brother, Trevor.

"That was a lot of fun," said Trevor. "But, man, he grabbed my gun. I had a hard time finding a toy gun that looked so real."

"Here, you can have mine," said Robby. He passed his gun to his brother. "I don't want it anyway." *Some guy might think it's real and shoot me to protect himself.*

"Thanks, bro. I don't know what I'd do without this baby. It looks so real that it brings me a lot of respect everywhere I point it."

Having been in town for only a few days, the boys found a friend in Damon Burke, whom they'd met their very first day in Forest Valley. Although Damon had helped them out by directing them to a seldom-used storage room where they could sleep and occasionally brought them food from home, he had a way of always getting into trouble. Because of that, he and Trevor had bonded. Trevor couldn't seem to stay out of trouble either, and Robby was beginning to second guess his decision to go with Trevor.

Damon flipped on his turn signal and rounded the corner. "Too bad we weren't able to grab that girl. She sure was a pretty little thing."

"What were you gonna do to her?" asked Robby.

Trevor laughed. "We weren't gonna do anything to her. We just wanted to take her out, treat her special, watch her give her boyfriend the slip."

"After one evening with us, she'd never go back to him," said Damon. "'Cause we were going to treat her like royalty."

With a sigh, Robby turned his attention to the scenery zipping past his side window. Sad as it was, he wasn't sure he believed them. He hadn't known Damon for very long, but he'd known Trevor his whole life. Yet, he doubted that his brother's intentions were honorable. Since they'd been in Forest Valley, he'd seen a side of Trevor he didn't know existed, and that bothered him. So he was glad that they'd attempted to pick up a girl whose guy had enough backbone to fight for her.

Damon spun the car into a downtown parking space. "Let's go find someone to annoy."

"Hey, how about that little shop owner that we pestered a couple of days ago?" asked Trevor.

With a month to go before his eighteenth birthday, Robby was still a minor, with no way to survive on his own. He left his home in Los Angeles, California, and traveled to Forest Valley, Wyoming, with his brother. He wanted to be with Trevor. He wanted to be like Trevor.

He wanted Trevor to accept him. But all Trevor wanted was to skate by at someone else's expense. Boy, would their mother be disappointed in them if she knew what they'd been doing.

Chapter 4

Decisions! Decisions!

As the little car disappeared from view, Skip kissed and embraced his trembling bride. "You all right?"

"I was never so scared. I thought they were going to shoot us."

"Not with this." Releasing Cassandra, Skip held up the gun. "It's a toy."

Cassandra looked up at him. "A toy! How did you know they only had toy guns?"

"I didn't. It's too dark to distinguish a toy from the real thing, but I wasn't about to let them force you into their car." Sliding his arm around her, Skip escorted her around to the passenger side of their car. "When I didn't respond to their orders in a way that they expected, they started to get nervous, which led me to the conclusion that it was just an act, and maybe the guns weren't even real."

After seating Cassandra, Skip jumped behind the wheel of the car, and they headed for town.

"Let's grab a bite to eat. I know where there's a great steakhouse." Skip shifted to second gear, and then to third.

"Skip, the car rolls so smoothly when you drive. How do you keep it from jerking?"

"Practice. And always let the clutch out slowly." As they cruised into town, Skip knew he had to run Cassandra out to her mother's house so she could pack up her bedroom, and this may be the only opportunity he'd have to take her. "After we eat, we'll run out to your mom's house so you can pack up and take home whatever you'll want to have at our house."

Cassandra looked at him in surprise. "Skip, I don't want to live with your family. I want us to have our own place. I thought this arrangement was only temporary until we got into our own little apartment."

"Well, it is only temporary," said Skip as he completed a right-hand turn. "Unfortunately, I don't know how temporary. Because my income supports my family, it's not really possible for us to simply move out on our own right now."

"But, Skip, you said …"

"… that it would be temporary." Skip completed her sentence. "I did say that, and it will be. But I didn't mean a week or two. It will more likely be a year or two."

Cassandra groaned. "That's not fair. I want to move into our own apartment. Come on, Skip, be reasonable."

Slowing the car to a stop at a red light, Skip pondered his mother's advice. One day she'd told him that marriage wasn't all fun and joy. There would be times that he and Cassandra would disagree adamantly about something, and it might be a challenge to work it out. But he didn't think it would happen so soon.

Skip sighed. "Well, Cassandra, we have a couple alternatives. If you'd prefer, you can still live with your mom and sister until I'm able to get out from under the financial responsibility of my family. Then, when I get my own apartment, you can move in with me, and we'll have our own place." Skip turned into a parking space downtown.

Cassandra looked at him. "I don't like that idea at all."

"Okay, how about this idea. You and I will go house shopping. Then my mom and sisters can move in with us. Then the house will be ours. And they can live with us."

Cassandra started laughing. "Skip, you come up with the most creative solutions. But I think it will be harder to get them out of our house than it will for us to move out of your mom's house when the time is right. So we'll just stay with your family for now."

Skip leaned over and kissed her. "Anything you say, Cassandra." Skip jumped out of the car and hurried around to open her door. "Come on. I'm starved."

Grasping her hand, he escorted her down the wide, downtown sidewalk, passing several stores on their way to the restaurant.

"So do you want me to run you to your mom's house after we eat so you can pack up a few things and bring them home with you?" asked Skip.

"No need. My room is already packed up. All we have to do is go and get everything. And it's organized and labeled, so I know where everything is. But with you going back to work tomorrow, I don't want to spend our only night together doing that. I have everything I need for now. We can run out there another day."

"Then let's catch a motel tonight so we can have some time alone."

"Skip, you have to work tomorrow."

With a heavy sigh, Skip angrily kicked a pebble into the street. "Don't remind me."

Since he'd left the house, he'd given it some serious thought. He needed to spend at least one night alone with his bride, and a motel would satisfy that need, but come morning, he'd have to run her home before heading to work unless he didn't mind paying for two nights in the motel.

Holding Cassandra's hand, Skip swung his arm as they sauntered down the downtown sidewalk. He could cover two nights. Maybe even three. A motel would be much quieter than his house. He had four active little sisters. His Aunt Rose was visiting his mother. Even though he had to work every day, staying at a motel would allow them a little solitude.

"Cassandra, we haven't had much time alone. Let's stay at a motel tonight."

With a grin, Cassandra caressed the back of his hand with her thumb. That thought appealed to her. She and Skip would be alone, even if only for one night. No interruptions. But what good would that do when he went to bed at nine o'clock? What did he expect her to do all evening? She couldn't even turn on the television because it would keep him awake. If they returned to his house, they wouldn't have the privacy, but at least she'd have someone to talk to after he went to bed, and she could watch television or even read in another room without the light disturbing him.

Cassandra sighed. "And what would we do at a motel? You have to work tomorrow, which means you have to be in bed at a decent hour. By the time we checked into a motel and got to our room, it would be your bedtime. Let's just go to your house."

"You mean our house. You live there now, too. At least until we get our own place."

That thought made Cassandra smile. *He is thinking of ways to get us into our own place.*

Without warning, a young man bolted from a nearby store and slammed into Skip, knocking him down and toppling onto him. Cassandra leaped aside as his two comrades raced out the door after him. The older boy tumbled over them, but the younger lad darted around them and took off. Scrambling to their feet, the boys dashed off.

"And don't come back." The store owner bounded into the doorway, waving his fist in the air.

Gasping for breath, Skip rolled to his side.

"Skip, are you hurt?" Cassandra knelt beside him.

The man set down his broom and stepped over to Skip. "You all right, son?"

Skip slowly sat up and nodded. "It's a good thing I hadn't eaten yet. What hit me?"

"You mean, who hit you?" said Cassandra.

Grasping his arms, Cassandra and the shopkeeper helped him to his feet.

"Ah, them lousy bums. They've been coming in my store for days now. They don't buy anything. They just aggravate me and chase away my customers."

Skip brushed off his clothes. "Have they stolen anything?"

"I don't think so. They're just nuisances."

"Have you filed a police report?"

"No, but if they don't cut it out, I'll have no choice."

Robby darted around the corner and jerked to a stop. Why was he running? He hadn't done anything wrong. The other two had tipped over the display and frightened those elderly ladies by their unruly behavior. Trevor and Damon raced past him and kept on running.

Peeking around the corner, Robby glanced back at the shop owner and young couple they'd terrorized just a short while ago. They stood there talking. No one was chasing him or his brother. The shop owner turned and went back into his store. Holding hands, the couple crossed the street and entered the steakhouse.

Steakhouse? That reminded him of food, and boy, was he hungry. He hadn't had a good meal in two days. Heading back to the small shop, Robby intended to give the owner an apology and help him pick up the mess that his brother made. But before he'd gone very far, his brother returned looking for him.

"Robby, come on," called Trevor. "Damon invited us to his house for a bite to eat."

"Eat?" echoed Robby. His stomach growled. Pivoting around, he followed his brother.

The last three days had been hectic, and Skip hadn't gotten much sleep. His wedding and ensuing honeymoon, if you could call it that, had been a blaze of adventure, and it was finally catching up with him. Skip yawned all the way through dinner.

"Tired, Angel?"

Removing his glasses, he rubbed his eyes. "Yeah, I'm really tired."

Cassandra squeezed his hand. "Come on. Let's go home."

This was their first real time alone together since they'd gotten married, and he was too tired to enjoy her company. That disappointed him. He couldn't imagine how she felt when he got called back to work so soon after the wedding. And to make matters worse, they weren't even going home to their own little apartment.

Leaving the restaurant, Skip seated his young bride in the car before sliding behind the wheel.

Cassandra lowered her window and turned on the radio. "Don't fall asleep, Skip."

Skip stifled another yawn. "I'm awake." Despite that declaration, it was well past his bedtime for a work night, and he could hardly keep his eyes open. He wouldn't have been so exhausted had he not missed so much sleep the past three nights, but Cassandra chattered all the way home. It was probably the only thing that kept him awake.

After a long, twenty-five minute drive from downtown, Skip finally turned into the driveway and parked beside his mother's mint green minivan. Sliding out of the car, he softly closed his door and hustled around to get his wife, motioning for her to be quiet.

"It's after eleven, and I don't want my mom to see us coming in."

"Why not?"

"Cause I feel ornery tonight. I guess I'm still upset that I have to work tomorrow. Anyway, I told her I'd be home in time to get ready for work."

"Did you leave her with the impression that we'd be out all night?"

"Yes, but I thought we'd crash at a motel, and I didn't want her to know because she wouldn't appreciate me spending money for that. So follow me quietly. I don't want to get caught breaking into my own house."

Chapter 5

A Prayer for Reconciliation

Crouching down, Skip ducked behind the cars as he crept around the side of the house and through the back gate. They entered the house through the back door of the two-story brick home. Cassandra followed him. Skip unlocked the door and pushed it open, thankful that the hinges didn't squeak.

He stepped into the kitchen and listened for his mother. The house was quiet, but a soft glow illuminated the kitchen. It was coming from the entranceway on the other side of the room.

Removing their shoes, the couple silently crossed the kitchen and slipped through the other doorway. Now in the large entranceway of the house, Skip heard his mother through the open living room doorway chatting with Aunt Rose. With a quick glance to his left, he ensured the front door was securely bolted before stealing up the polished, hardwood stairs to his right, Cassandra right behind him. Once inside Skip's room, they closed the door and flipped on the light.

"How about that?" said Skip. "I can't believe we did it. My mom has radar ears."

Stepping silently to his dresser, he opened the top drawer and pulled out an envelope, handing it to Cassandra.

"What's this?" Cassandra opened it and gasped. "One hundred dollar savings bonds. Skip, where did you get them?" She emptied them into her hand and fanned them out. "There are six."

Skip unbuttoned his shirt and slipped it off. "My dad bought one for me every year on my birthday. I had sixteen, but I cashed in ten of them to help pay for our rings and to have some ready cash on our honeymoon. But we didn't have a chance to spend any money, so I still have five hundred dollars." Skip stepped out of his trousers and pulled on his blue striped pajamas.

Dropping them back into the envelope, Cassandra laid it on the dresser and quickly changed into her mint-colored silk nightgown. "It's late, and you have to work tomorrow. Set the alarm, and let's go to bed."

Sitting on the comfortable living room sofa, Rose chatted softly with Erin. She found her sister-in-law to be a warm and loving person. How could she have let a grudge keep her from talking to her brother and meeting his family all these years? And over something so ridiculous.

At age eighteen, she left home with hopes and dreams and a business idea that would make her extremely wealthy. But she felt that Forest Valley, Wyoming, was too small to build her empire, so she headed to the big city. And she begged Stephen to go with her. They would get rich together. After all, he was her very best friend.

Only problem was, he loved Forest Valley, and nothing could get him to leave. The last time she saw him, there was sadness in his eyes that she would never forget. It looked like he'd lost his best friend, and she knew that it grieved him that she left with bitterness against him because he wouldn't go with her.

Stephen had written her dozens of letters that she never answered. She knew that he'd gotten married and had a son. He wrote to her for ten years after she stormed out on him. Finally, the letters stopped coming, but although Rose was no longer angry with him, she was too busy building her business and taking care of her family to even notice that he'd stopped writing.

Then two years ago, she buried her beloved husband after a year-long battle with cancer. But when her precious sons abandoned her, she thought of Stephen and knew if anyone could give her sound advice and guidance, it would be her brother. So she purchased an airline ticket and flew home, only to learn this morning when she arrived that her brother had died four years earlier.

If it hadn't been for her nephew, who happened to be at the airport picking up his little sister, Rose would have turned right around and headed back to LA. But Skip insisted that she come home with him and meet the whole family. Now she was glad she had. Her only regret was that she hadn't come to her senses sooner and reconciled with her brother before he died. How wonderful it would have been for her boys to know Stephen and his family.

Erin Shaughnessy visited with Rose over a late-night cup of coffee. Although it was nearly midnight, Erin enjoyed the company way too much to call it a night. She'd known Rose for less than twelve hours, but this evening she felt like she was re-connecting with a sister that she hadn't seen in years. Stephen had always spoken very highly of Rose, and he had often prayed that God would help them to reconcile. And although he wasn't there to see it, four years after he went to be with the Lord, God still answered his prayer.

"Oh, Rose, you've been through so much these past two years." Erin hugged her. "Is there anything I can do to help you?"

Rose sighed. "Your friendship and understanding mean more to me than you'll ever know, because getting to know you has made me feel close to Stephen."

"Do you have any idea where your boys went when they ran off?" asked Erin.

"They came here, to Forest Valley. But Trevor is nineteen, and although Robby is still a minor, he's so close to legal age that it doesn't pay to drag him home, even if I could locate him."

"Do you worry about them getting into trouble? Drugs? Gangs? Any type of run-ins with the police?"

Rose shook her head. "No. Robby's pretty sensible. And Trevor may be stubborn and impulsive, but I can't see him doing anything illegal. However, I wish he were more like your son. Skip is responsible and settled."

"He is now, but he wasn't always like that. Skip was headstrong and determined to follow his own path."

"What changed him?"

"The death of his father. It forced him to take on a responsibility that he just couldn't ignore. Even then, it still took him three years to let go of the bitterness and anger he held against the man who killed Stephen. God did a miraculous work in his heart and life."

Rose sighed. "That's what Trevor needs. He's bitter against me. He says that I'm trying to run his life and that I favor his brother."

"Do you?"

Rose paused, obviously in thought. "Heavens, no. Trevor's angry because I won't buy him everything he wants. I certainly have the money to. But despite my success, Gary and I tried to teach both our boys good work ethics. Robby grasped the lessons early in life, but Trevor doesn't see why he should have to work for a living when I'm wealthy. And since I favor his brother's good attitude and praise him for his level of independence, he sees that as favoring his brother.”

With a yawn, Erin slowly got to her feet. “I can hardly keep my eyes open, and I know you’ve had a very long day. Let's go to bed. We’ll talk more tomorrow.”

“Where am I sleeping?” Rose grasped the hard plastic handle of her large suitcase, pulled it up, and tipped her suitcase onto the two wheels, drawing it behind her as she followed Erin toward the stairs.

Erin blinked at the sight of the suitcase. “Oh, Rose, I’m so sorry. I should have asked Skip to carry that up the stairs for you.”

Reaching the foot of the stairs, Rose pushed down the handle, tipped the suitcase onto its side, and grasped the side carry handle. “That’s all right. I’ve done it before. I can do it again.” Rose dragged the heavy suitcase up the stairs on its side, sliding it up one step at a time. When she finally reached the top, she once again set her suitcase upright and pulled out the handle to wheel it behind her. Rose looked up and down the dimly lit hallway. “Which way?”

“Well, since Skip and Cassandra aren't coming home tonight, you can sleep in their bed.” Erin escorted her down the hall to Skip's closed bedroom door. “Goodness, why’s the door closed?” She quietly turned the knob and pushed open the door. The hallway light illuminated the bedroom, and Erin’s mouth dropped open when she saw that Skip was in bed sound asleep, Cassandra in his arms.

“Isn't that sweet?” whispered Rose.

"Heavens, how did they get into the house without us hearing them?"

"I guess I'll sleep downstairs on the sofa tonight."

Erin closed the door and started toward her bedroom at the other end of the hallway. "No, you won't. I have a king-sized bed. Why don't you share with me tonight?"

"Are you sure, Erin? We barely know each other." Rose trailed her as they passed the stairs and entered the master bedroom.

"Yet, I feel a great relationship building between us. Something tells me that this evening was the start of a wonderful friendship."

Rose parked her suitcase up against the far wall and opened it, pulling out her pink pajamas and a personal hygiene bag. The ladies chatted softly as they got ready for bed.

"Erin, how did Stephen die?"

"He picked up Skip from baseball practice, and they were on their way home. Stephen stopped by a convenience store to grab a drink for Skip, and he walked in on a robbery in progress. The robber shot him. Skip saw everything through the front glass window of the store."

Rose gasped. "Oh, Erin, I'm so sorry! No wonder he was so full of bitterness. How can you be sure that he's overcome it? A lot of people repress painful memories and emotions for years."

"One night he had an encounter with God. The Lord cleansed his heart of all bitterness, enabling him to forgive the man that killed his father."

Rose shook her head. "I don't know, Erin. An experience like that is so traumatic that most people harbor grudges for years and aren't even aware of it."

"Trust me, Skip is free from it."

"How can you be so certain?"

"Are you sure you can handle it, Rose? Your brother was murdered, and this information will affect you."

Rose sighed. "Right now, nothing seems as distressing as the knowledge of how far my boys have wandered from the Lord."

"Then follow me." Erin led Rose back to Skip's room and pushed open the door. The hallway light softly illuminated the room as the ladies peeked in. Skip and Cassandra didn't stir.

"What is it, Erin? I don't get it."

"That girl, Rose. She is the daughter of the man that killed Stephen. She is a constant reminder of who killed his dad."

Rose's mouth fell open. "That's incredible. How did their relationship come about under those circumstances?"

"Neither of them knew when they started dating. By the time they realized it, they were in love."

Chapter 6

Pondering Circumstances

With a yawn, Skip reached over Cassandra and switched off his alarm clock before dragging his tired body out of bed. He wished he could snuggle up beside her and go back to sleep. He wanted to forget he had to work today. Surely they didn't need him that badly.

Skip rubbed the sleep from his eyes and collected some clean clothes, shuffling down the hallway into the bathroom still half asleep. Maybe a hot shower would help. Despite going to bed three hours past his bedtime on a work night, the shower stimulated him just enough to wake him up. Hopefully, it was enough to help him survive the long duty day.

Slipping into the bedroom, Skip brushed his lips against the soft cheek of his sleeping mate and quietly left for work.

Normally, the twenty-five minute commute didn't bother him, but today he didn't appreciate the long drive. His honeymoon had been canceled. His vacation had been interrupted. His sleep had been cut short. And his bride would spend the day without him. To top it all off, he'd probably pull a sixteen-hour day. The thought of it did not help his disposition in the slightest.

Skip spun his blue Buick sedan into the police station parking lot and parked beside Jesse's beat up red Ford pickup truck. He cut the engine and sat there for a moment. With a heavy sigh, he crossed his arms over the steering wheel, closed his eyes, and rested his head on his arms.

"Lord, I'm angry. This isn't fair to me or to Cassandra. I'm sorry for my attitude. I'm going to need Your help to get through the day." Pulling himself together, Skip stepped from his car and quietly entered the station. The instant he walked into the locker room, Officer Jesse Spencer hailed him.

"Good morning, Skip."

Jesse's salutation irritated Skip even more, but he plastered on a smile and returned his partner's greeting. "Hi, Jesse."

It was a mere six days before his twentieth birthday, and Skip had been with the Forest Valley Police Department for nearly two years. With great difficulty, the chief of police managed to obtain approval from the Wyoming state governor and overcome objections from city council to waive the minimum age requirement, allowing Skip to join the department right out of high school.

Because of Skip's youth, Captain Paul Kramer kept him partnered with his field training officer the entire time. That was Jesse. But the department was simply spread too thin today. As a result, Kramer separated them and gave Skip his own car. That's when Skip realized how badly they needed him.

During briefing, Captain Kramer mentioned the three youthful offenders that had gone on a rampage through the streets of Forest Valley.

"They're mostly an annoyance, finding new ways to bother people. But we need to locate them and put a halt to their shenanigans before somebody gets hurt. Have any of you guys crossed paths with them?"

Skip swallowed hard, but remained silent. He knew that he should tell about his encounters with them the night before. After all, they had attempted to kidnap Cassandra with toy guns. Kidnapping was a felony, but a stunt like that could get them killed because they would eventually threaten someone with a real gun who would shoot them, not knowing that they were only wielding toys.

"Does anybody know anything about them?" asked Kramer. "We still haven't gotten a decent description of any of these boys. They must have some type of vehicle, because they certainly get around."

Skip pursed his lips and glanced away. He didn't want to discuss last night's incident. At the moment he wanted to melt into the woodwork and disappear. But he knew his irritation would dissipate once he hit the street. He loved this job.

"Skip, are you all right?" asked Kramer.

"Yes, sir." Skip looked up at him.

"That's all I've got," said Captain Kramer, addressing first shift. "Keep your eyes peeled for these hoods. Grab radios and move out."

Skip slowly got to his feet and migrated towards the back of the room. As the officers grabbed fully-charged radios to get them through the day, they filed into the hallway and headed toward the back door of the police station. Jesse followed Skip through the doorway and pulled him aside.

"What's the matter with you this morning?" he demanded.

Skip raised an eyebrow. Jesse knew him well. Could he have figured out that Skip had already had a run-in with those three boys and could identify them? *Great.* First shift would laugh at him when they learned that Cassandra almost got kidnapped by a guy with a toy gun.

"Look, pal, I know you're upset about having to work today, but you'd better pay closer attention on the street than you did in briefing or you won't have to worry about coming to work tomorrow because we'll be burying you." Without waiting for a reply, his comrade spun on his heel and strode out the back door.

For a moment, Skip just stood there, stung by Jesse's harshness. *Boy is he cranky this morning.*

Following him out the door, Skip jumped into his patrol car and turned out of the station parking lot, pondering his friend's outburst. Then he remembered that Jesse had transferred from another department after his best friend was killed. Jesse and Skip were more than partners. They were best friends.

Coasting to a stop at a red light, Skip rested his elbow on the open window ledge and propped his head on his hand.

And like half the department, Jesse is pulling double shifts. He's put in some long hours. No wonder he's on edge.

The instant the light changed, Skip accelerated through the intersection, but almost immediately, he slowed to a stop behind a tremendously long line of cars. The next traffic light was nearly a quarter mile up the road. What was holding up traffic? An accident?

Just then, dispatch radioed Skip, alerting him to a collision between a motorist and a bicyclist on Brookhurst Boulevard.

Well, that's what's holding up traffic. Flipping on his lights, he carefully maneuvered his patrol car around stopped traffic and coasted down the shoulder of the road.

As he neared the accident, the dispatch officer informed him that an ambulance had already been dispatched.

Skip stopped on the shoulder and jumped out of his car, trotting over to a crowd of adults who lingered in the middle of the street. Almost immediately, they moved aside, allowing him through. A young boy, no older than nine or ten, lay in the middle of the street.

Good gracious, what is a child this young doing outside at this early hour? And why's he riding his bicycle on a main road?

Catching sight of the Forest Valley three-some from the night before, he jerked to a stop. The two older boys stood gaping at the injured child while the youngest lad squatted beside him, covering him with a blanket.

Recognition dawned on their faces as their eyes met Skip's. The two trouble-makers turned to run, but they found themselves surrounded by an ever-growing crowd of early morning commuters. In a near panic, the boys seized their young friend and jerked him to his feet before shoving their way out and disappearing into the crowd.

Skip wanted to chase after them, but his priority was the injured child. Besides, by the time he jostled his way through the gathering of concerned on-lookers, those boys would be long gone.

Chapter 7

Baseball and the Bride

Skip squatted beside the unconscious boy. He lifted the blanket long enough to check for obvious injuries, like bleeding or compound fractures. He felt for the child's pulse and checked his respiration. The boy was going into shock, so Skip re-covered him.

Rising to his feet, he glanced around the crowd of people. "Who was driving?"

A trembling middle-aged man stepped forward. He was white as a sheet. It was obvious to Skip that it took every ounce of his courage to not run from the accident. He was terrified after hitting a child with his car.

"Does anyone know this child?" asked Skip.

Everyone shook their heads. No one knew him.

Skip requested that anyone who was not involved or hadn't witnessed the incident to go on their way. That cleared out a lot of people, leaving him to talk to the driver and two witnesses who were willing to give a statement. After checking the man's driver's license and auto insurance, Skip separated him from the witnesses and asked him what happened.

"I ... I was driving along this road when he came flying out into traffic from between two parked cars, and I simply couldn't stop in time. I mean, all of a sudden he was in front of my car."

"What about the three fellows that just left here? Were they involved somehow?"

"No. After I hit that little boy, I was going to move him out of the road, but one of those boys stopped me. He checked the kid's breathing, stopped the bleeding, and treated him for shock. I'm glad they stopped to help because I didn't know what to do."

While they talked, the ambulance arrived.

"But only the youngest one actually helped the child. Is that right?"

The man nodded.

"So he wasn't moved at all?" asked Skip.

"No, officer, that young man said he could have a back or neck injury."

Skip took statements from his two witnesses, thankful that they corroborated the driver's story. That made it easy for him. Allowing the driver and witnesses to leave the scene, he directed traffic while the paramedics prepared the boy for transport to the hospital.

When the ambulance finally pulled away, Skip sat in his cruiser jotting down notes while everything was fresh in his mind. Finally, he keyed his mic and informed dispatch that he was back in service. Immediately, they dispatched him to take a theft complaint at a private residence.

Skip acknowledged the call before pulling out into traffic and heading for the address of the complainant. Ten minutes later, he parked in front of a ranch-style brick house, grabbed his one-inch thick metal clip board, and hiked up the driveway toward the front door.

A woman dashed out the door and met him halfway. "I feel like a fool, calling the police about this, but I've had all I can take."

"You reported a theft?" asked Skip.

"Come. I'll show you."

Skip followed her into the backyard.

"There. You see?" She motioned toward her apple tree. "It used to be full. But just when the apples get ripe enough to eat, they disappear. So I started watching out my window."

"Did you see who's picking them?" asked Skip.

"I sure did. There were three of them. A boy about sixteen or seventeen and a couple of older fellows – maybe nineteen."

"Hmm." From the compartment in his clip board, Skip withdrew the paperwork he'd need to complete a theft report, clipped it onto his board, and started writing. "When did this happen?"

"Oh, it just happened maybe twenty minutes ago."

Skip glanced at his watch. "About 9:05?"

"Yes."

"Can you describe them?"

The woman thought for a moment. Then she relayed the details she could recall about the boys involved. Skip knew from her description that these were definitely the same guys that just left the scene of the accident.

They wasted no time in getting here. They must have already known the location of that apple tree.

"When did your apples start disappearing?"

"I first noticed it about a week ago. So every day I've been watching, and today I caught them in the act. I yelled at those boys when I saw them, and they ran."

Skip grinned. "They usually do. If you see them again, don't let them know that you're watching them. Just pick up the phone and call us right away."

"But if I do that, they'll get away with all my apples."

"They might, but we might catch them, too. If you holler at them first, I guarantee they'll get away with some of your apples, and we'll never catch them."

"All right. Next time I'll call you right away."

When Cassandra awoke, she yawned and stretched before sitting up in bed. *Oh, what a nice dream that was.* She and Skip were walking through the park holding hands.

Glancing around the quiet room, it suddenly looked very unfamiliar. Everything was out of place. Cassandra frowned and looked around.

Wait a minute. Everywhere she looked, she saw baseball. Baseball pictures. Baseball trophies. Baseball paraphernalia on the dresser. *Where are my pictures and my bookcase and my dresser. These things aren't mine.*

Suddenly it hit her. She wasn't in her room. She was in Skip's room. Cassandra sighed, and tears welled up in her eyes. She now lived with his family. And all she had the time to bring with her was one small suitcase.

Sliding off the full-sized bed, Cassandra dropped her suitcase onto it and opened it up. She pulled out a pair of blue denim capris and a pink v-neck shirt. Re-closing her suitcase, she set it in the corner of Skip's room and hurriedly dressed before making the bed. Slipping into her tennis shoes, she quietly headed into the hallway and down the stairs, feeling like a guest in someone else's home.

Cassandra followed the sound of voices into the kitchen.

"Well, good morning, sleepy head," said Erin. She and Rose were enjoying a cup of coffee at the breakfast table. "What time did you and Skip get in last night?"

"Oh, probably about 11:30."

"Did Skip go to work this morning?"

"Yeah. He wasn't happy about it, but he went." Cassandra dropped onto a dining room chair and blinked back a tear.

"Looks like you're not happy about it, either," said Rose.

Cassandra sighed. "I'm not. But it's worse having to be *here.*"

Erin raised an eyebrow.

"I'm ... I'm sorry," said Cassandra. "I didn't mean it like that. Honest."

Erin patted her hand. "Not to worry. Let's see what we can do about that? First, let's go check out your living arrangements."

Not sure what she meant, Cassandra followed the ladies up the stairs and into Skip's room.

Rose put a finger to her chin. "Hmm, this room definitely needs a woman's touch. I see way too much sports in here."

"Oh, no," exclaimed Cassandra. "I am not about to touch his baseball possessions."

"Well, ya know, Cassandra, now that you're married, you need to consider Skip," said Erin. "It's no longer just about your needs and your wants."

"That's exactly what I'm doing," said Cassandra.

"But what about Skip?" asked Rose. "Now that he's married, he needs to consider you. It's no longer all about his needs and his wants. In fact, as far as Skip is concerned, it's never been about his needs and his wants. That's why he stayed home to care for his widowed mother and four young sisters."

Erin nodded. "So now that he's married, he also has a wife to consider – your needs and your wants. Do you think for even a minute, he'd be upset if you brought some of your things from home and found a place for them in this room?"

Cassandra smiled. "No, I don't."

"Then we'd better get moving, because we have a lot of work to do," said Rose.

"And then we have a birthday party to plan," added Erin. "Stephanie will be ten on Sunday, and Skip will turn twenty next Tuesday."

The ladies hurried back down to the kitchen. Cassandra poured herself a cup of coffee and grabbed a muffin while Erin called Ruth, the next door neighbor, asking if she could watch the girls for a couple of hours. Ruth was delighted to keep them, as always. So within twenty minutes, Erin's young daughters ran next door to visit while the ladies piled into Erin's mint-green minivan and took off for Anita McKenzie's house, the home of Cassandra's mother.

"Cassandra, won't your mother be at work at this hour?" asked Erin.

"Yeah, but Melanie should be home. And if for some reason she's not, I still have a key."

Almost thirty minutes later, Erin pulled into the driveway and Cassandra led the way. She entered the house without knocking, so she called to her sister.

"Melanie, it's me. Just stopping by to pick up some things."

"Okay," yelled Melanie from another room.

Cassandra escorted the ladies upstairs to her bedroom. There were boxes stacked everywhere. "I know I can't take them all ..."

"Of course, you can," said Erin. "Now, this may be too much for us to carry down today. But over the next couple of weeks, we can move it all over to our house."

"But where would we put it?" asked Cassandra.

Erin draped her arm around Cassandra and drew her into a gentle hug. "You may not be aware of this because the door is always closed, however, there is another bedroom at the end of the hall. It's mostly used for storage. But knowing that you and Skip would need the room, Skip and I cleaned out that room a couple of weeks ago, so it's totally empty. You'll have lots of room for your things. And while Skip is at work, Aunt Rose and I will help you get organized and rearrange everything to make Skip's room your bridal suite. Because our home is now your home."

Chapter 8

Skip Gets Drafted

Leaving the case of the disappearing apples unresolved, Skip responded to another radio call. Then another and another. For the next three hours, he was running from one call to another.

When his radio finally fell silent, he drove to one of the busiest streets in town and parked, observing traffic while he relaxed for a few minutes. He wondered how long he'd have before the next wave hit.

With his window rolled down, he rested his arm on the ledge, deep in thought. The actions of the three young men disturbed him. They harassed store owners, yet aided the child at the scene of the accident. They drove around in a fairly new car, but apparently had to steal food to eat.

Another patrol car pulled up beside him, facing the opposite direction. Jesse lowered his window. "Hey, Skip, let's meet for lunch at Becky's Beacon. My treat. The captain's meeting us there 'cause he wants to talk to you."

"Hmm?" Skip started to respond but caught sight of the little white Datsun. Without acknowledging Jesse, he flipped on his turn signal and pulled out into traffic.

Not wanting the driver of the Datsun to know he was being tailed, Skip followed from a distance. After traveling several blocks and making various turns, the driver pulled over to the curb and let out the other two boys.

Skip casually drove past them, taking note of the car's license number. Pulling around the corner into a narrow alley, he jotted down the number while it was fresh in his mind. Re-pocketing his small spiral notebook, he looked up just in time to see the two young men through his rear view mirror. They rounded the corner and jerked to a stop at the sight of a police car. Their mouths dropped open, and all color left their cheeks. Twirling around, the boys bolted in opposite directions.

Skip watched them run off and simply shook his head. Putting the car in gear, he drove around the block and onto the main road. His growling stomach reminded him it was almost lunchtime, so he glanced around to see what restaurants were close by. He considered all his favorite places, hoping the radio remained quiet long enough for him to grab a bite to eat.

"Hmm, now what am I in the mood for?" Then it hit him that Jesse had pulled up right beside him and invited him to lunch at Becky's Beacon. But he was so determined to catch those three hoodlums that he drove off without saying a word. "Oh, man. How could I do that to Jesse? I was so rude."

Turning the corner, Skip headed for Becky's Beacon. "I'd better radio Jesse." Just as he reached for his mic, Captain Kramer's crisp voice grabbed his attention.

"Shaughnessy, meet me at Becky's Beacon."

Skip grabbed his mic. "Yes, sir. I'm three minutes out." While he still had the mic in his hand, Skip radioed dispatch of his code seven location. That way, he wouldn't get flagged to handle any radio calls while he was at lunch.

When Skip turned into the parking lot of Becky's Beacon, he spotted two other cruisers in the lot. He hoped that one of them belonged to Jesse because he owed his friend an apology.

With an embarrassed grin, Skip joined the other two officers. "Sorry, Jesse. I was a little preoccupied when you pulled in beside me, and it only registered a minute ago."

"That's all right. Have a seat." Jesse slid over and Skip sat down beside him. "You hungry? My offer is still open. Besides, I owe you an apology for snapping at you this morning, but I got concerned when you didn't pay attention during briefing."

"I was paying attention."

Sitting across from Skip and Jesse, Kramer raised an eyebrow. "I agree with Jesse. You looked distracted this morning during briefing. Is there something you would like to share with us?"

"No, sir."

Jesse flagged down a waitress and ordered Skip some lunch.

"Okay, Skip," said Kramer. "Now I have a favor to ask you. Johnny has been working hard to organize a baseball team for some of the troubled youth in our area."

"Isn't Johnny in the hospital?" asked Skip.

Kramer nodded. "He intended to draft you to help him with this project as soon as you returned from your honeymoon, but now he's in no condition to see it through. Would you be willing to take over for him? Jesse can help you."

"Is this during duty hours?" asked Skip.

"Afraid not. I can't spare anyone right now. This is on your own time."

"What time? I thought everyone was pulling sixteen-hour days."

"Well, with you and a couple other guys well enough to return to work, we have enough people to split the station into two shifts. As of today, everyone is on twelve hours."

The waitress brought Skip's lunch and he shoveled it down while they talked.

"If these kids are on the verge of serving jail time, they'll resent me because of my age. Johnny needs someone they'll respect."

"That's true, but you're the best ball player with the department. Johnny said you almost signed a contract with a major league team."

"I wish Johnny would quit telling people that."

"It's not true?" asked Kramer.

"Yeah, it's true. I just wish he'd stop announcing it."

"Will you do it, Skip?"

Skip glanced at his partner and back at his captain. "If I have some help to maintain discipline. 'Cause I don't want to face ten or twelve troublemakers by myself."

Captain Kramer looked at Jesse.

"I'll be his backup."

"Great. You guys finish your lunch, and then hop over to the hospital to see Johnny. He can tell you where he is on this project."

When Skip finished eating, he jumped into his cruiser and took off for the hospital, Jesse right behind him. He flew through yellow lights to get to the hospital as fast as he could. To his surprise, Jesse followed him through on red.

Although he and Jesse were best friends, he considered Johnny his big brother. Johnny was a family friend who had known Erin and Stephen since Skip was a baby. It was Johnny's bold request that drove Chief Clark to petition the governor, allowing Skip to join the department two years younger than the minimum age requirement.

Pulling into the hospital parking lot, the officers met in the lobby and took the elevator up to Johnny's room. Johnny's hospital room door stood wide open. Pausing right outside the door, Skip knocked softly before leading the way into the room.

Johnny smiled when he saw them. "Hi, fellows. Hey, kid, what are you doing here? I thought you weren't due back until next week."

Ever since he could remember, Johnny had called him 'kid.'

"Yeah, so did I." Skip sighed and slid his hands into his pockets.

"Hey, where's Pete? Is he in another room?" asked Jesse

"Pete went home this morning, and I'm bored with no one to talk to."

"You have any idea when they'll release you?" asked Skip.

"They're talking about keeping me until next week."

Skip whistled softly. "Boy, are you a mess."

Johnny had two black eyes and a bruised face. An ace wrap covered his forehead. His left arm was in a sling.

"What happened?"

"We were clobbered by a pick-up truck that ran a red light. The driver was killed and the car we were chasing got away."

"Did you catch the license plate number?" asked Skip.

"Unfortunately, no, but the car was a little white Datsun."

Skip raised an eyebrow. "Really? What were they wanted for?"

"Reckless driving," said Johnny. "The driver was weaving in and out of traffic like he was trying to get away from the police car. So I flipped on my lights and took off after him. That's when the chase actually started. But I was too far away to catch his license plate number."

"Well, if there's anything we can do for you, let us know," said Jesse.

"Actually, there is," said Johnny. "I've been organizing a baseball team for the troubled kids in our area – trying to keep them out of trouble, out of jail, and give them something constructive to occupy their time. But I'm currently indisposed because of my injuries."

"We can see that," said Skip. "What would you like us to do?"

With painful effort, Johnny slowly reached for the nightstand beside his bed. Pulling open the drawer, he carefully withdrew a piece of notebook paper and handed it to Skip. "Here, kid, my list of boys, complete with phone numbers and addresses."

Folding the paper, Skip slid it into his pocket.

"Now, don't lose that," instructed Johnny. "That's the only record I have."

"I'll take care of it. Anything else you need to tell us?"

"Good luck, fellows. You're going to need it." Johnny looked at Jesse. "And thanks for helping Skip with this project. 'Cause there's no way that he would be able to handle those kids alone."

"Well, we've got to get back on patrol," said Jesse.

Skip grasped Johnny's hand and gave it a gentle squeeze. "See you later."

The boys left Johnny's hospital room and rode the elevator down to the first floor. Jesse headed out the door, but Skip detoured to the emergency room, asking about the little boy that had been brought in early that morning.

"His name is Billy Watkins," said Emily, the lady at the registration desk. "He was admitted with two broken bones and a concussion, so he'll be all right. It took some doing, but we finally located his parents. They're with him now."

"Did you ever find out why that little guy was riding his bicycle at that hour?"

"He was running away from home. Apparently, his mom and dad had separated, and he was angry that he had to stay with his mother. So he took off early in the morning to go live with his dad."

"Thanks, Emily. Well, I got to run." With a quick wave, Skip left the hospital.

Reaching his patrol car, he ran a license check on the number he had copied down earlier. The little white Datsun was registered to Mrs. Leila Burke. Skip jotted down her address and headed to her house.

Chapter 9

The Bedroom

Transformation

Located in a run-down part of town, the small, white ranch-style house was in dire need of repair. It had broken shutters, along with chipped and peeling paint. It was missing whole pieces of siding. Roof shingles were sticking out of the overgrown shrubbery and sprinkled around the small lawn of six-inch tall weeds and crabgrass.

With no driveway, Skip parked at the curb and stepped from his patrol car. Immediately, all neighborhood activity stopped as everyone watched to see where he was going.

Striding up the front walk, he rapped on the door with his knuckles. No answer. He knocked again. Still no answer. Skip peered through the dirty front window to see if anyone even lived there or if the house was vacant.

A boy on a bicycle rode up to him and stopped. "They're going to get arrested all ready?"

Skip looked down at him. The lad was about twelve years old. "What do you mean, 'all ready?'"

"Well, they only moved in two or three weeks ago."

"Is that so? Do you know them?"

The boy shook his head. "The lady works all day. I see her car coming home at six o'clock every night."

"Does she live alone?" asked Skip.

"She has a son, but I've never seen anyone else, so I think it's just them two. Did they break the law?"

"No. I just want to ask them some questions. Thanks for your help." Skip returned to his car. The boy waved at him as he pulled away from the curb.

Since Leila Burke didn't get home until he got off work, he would have to stop by when he was off duty, but he couldn't come back this evening because it was a church night. He would drop by tomorrow after six.

It had been a busy morning for the ladies. Finally arriving home, they began the task of unloading the van and hauling the boxes upstairs and into the empty room. Stephanie and seven-year-old Sandy ran from Ruth's house to help them carry in whatever they could.

Pulling the last item out of the van, Erin handed it to Sandy.

"A white teddy bear," cried Sandy. "With a pretty blue ribbon around its neck." She hugged it. "Mom, it's so pretty. Can I have it?"

"I'm afraid it's not mine to give you, honey. It belongs to Cassandra. You run it upstairs and give it to her, while I go next door to pick up your little sisters. Then, come back downstairs and we'll make lunch for everyone."

"Okay."

Cassandra looked at all the boxes they'd stacked against the wall and heaved a sigh. "This is overwhelming. Where do I even begin?"

At that moment, Sandy ran up to her with a teddy bear. "Here, Cassandra. Here's your pretty teddy bear."

Tears sprang into her eyes as she gently took the bear from her young sister-in-law and hugged it. Just the sight of that bear made her think of Skip. "Thanks, Sandy."

As the child left the room, Cassandra looked at Rose. "I don't remember putting this bear in the van. I thought I left it sitting on the dresser."

"You did. I grabbed it. I saw the way you kept looking at it and knew it had a lot of sentimental value to you."

"It does. Skip won this bear for me last fall at the school festival."

"I suspected it was something like that. I'm glad I grabbed it for you. Now let's take a break and go help Erin prepare lunch," said Rose. "Then we'll get to work organizing your things and rearranging Skip's room to accommodate his new bride.

After lunch, Cassandra and Rose headed back up the stairs to get things organized. Erin put the little ones down for a nap before joining them. Skip had an extra dresser in his room, and it was totally empty.

"Wow! This is a gorgeous dresser," said Cassandra. "But there's nothing in it. That makes no sense."

"Oh, he bought that for you," said Erin. "He knew you'd need your own space for things. He has a friend that owns a furniture store, and he gave it to Skip for cost."

They worked all afternoon, rearranging the furniture, unboxing Cassandra's clothes and arranging them in the dresser drawers, making space for things in the closet and hanging up her dresses.

"Look at the curtains I bought for our bedroom," said Cassandra. The colorful curtains looked like a garden of flowers. "Aren't these pretty? You think Skip will mind?"

"If you're happy, he'll be happy," said Erin. "Besides, he doesn't even have any curtains up. Just a window shade."

When the ladies finally finished for the afternoon, Cassandra sighed with contentment as she admired the transformation of Skip's bachelor baseball bedroom into a delightful newly-wed bedroom, displaying some of her treasures alongside his.

"You think Skip will be okay with this?" asked Cassandra.

"He'd better," replied Aunt Rose. "His whole life changed the moment he said 'I do.' And I'm certain he knows that."

Chapter 10

Surprise! Surprise!

Skip was running from one call to another practically all day. And then he had reports to write. He didn't get off work early enough to head home before church. In fact, he didn't even have time to change clothes or grab a bite to eat. He would barely make it there by seven. But he loved the mid-week Bible study, so he headed out the door in uniform and drove straight to church, knowing that the rest of his family would already be there.

Skip entered the sanctuary three bars into the opening hymn of the service. He was late, but since everyone was standing and singing, he felt less awkward strolling down the aisle to the family pew, where he squeezed past Stephanie to stand beside Cassandra.

"Are you through for the day?" she whispered.

Skip nodded. Sharing her hymnal, he finished the song with the congregation.

The music director led the people attending worship right into a second song before turning the microphone over to the pastor.

Pastor Victor Greene bounded onto the platform as the parishioners took their seats. "For those of you who aren't aware, among our first time visitors is a newlywed couple."

Skip cringed and slid down in the pew as the pastor's comment caused heads to turn all over the auditorium. Cassandra, on the other hand, beamed at the recognition, and she sat up straighter.

"They were supposed to be on their honeymoon," added Pastor Greene. "But they're back early. Stand up, you two."

Cassandra bounded to her feet, but Skip wanted to crawl under the pew.

"Come on, Skip, stand up," said the preacher. "I'd like you both to come up here. I have something for you."

Cassandra grasped Skip's hand, pulled him to his feet, and pushed him past Stephanie into the aisle. Suddenly the center of attention, Skip found the situation embarrassing enough without his young bride leading him to the platform like a child. Twisting out of her grasp, he placed his left hand in the small of her back and took the lead away from her by escorting her up the aisle and onto the platform.

Pastor Greene greeted them both with a firm handshake. "Since this is a gift from your church family, I thought it appropriate to present it to you before the congregation. The church wanted to give you and Cassandra a wedding shower, but due to your living circumstances, we didn't feel that it was practical. So they took up a love offering last Sunday while you two were gone."

Cassandra smiled, and Skip relaxed until he glanced over at his family. His mouth fell open at the sight of Cassandra's sister, Melanie, and her mother, Anita McKenzie, sitting next to his mom. He'd been inviting them to church for a year, and he could never get them to come or even allow him to share the gospel with them. But he was thrilled to see them in church.

Shifting his gaze to Aunt Rose, who sat on the other side of his mother, Skip cringed at her look of shock. It had to be his uniform. He had forgotten to tell her that he was a cop.

Pastor Greene interrupted his thoughts. "Skip, there's so much a young married couple needs. So here is a check from all of us." He handed it to Skip and shook his hand again.

Skip's face got warm, and he suspected he might be blushing. "Thank you," he said into the microphone. "We appreciate your thoughtfulness." Still holding Cassandra's hand, he led her back to their seats.

"And, Erin, don't let that boy spend it on his little sisters."

"Not a dime."

The Surprise Family Union

Laughter erupted all over the auditorium.

After the service, the sanctuary was chaotic as people flocked around Skip and Cassandra to welcome them home. Anita and Melanie joined the cluster of friends hugging Cassandra.

Skip's stomach growled. It was past eight o'clock, and he hadn't eaten since noon. He was starved. He could slip out with Cassandra and they could sneak off alone to grab a bite to eat, but he knew that his little sisters had missed him tremendously and would be hurt if he didn't invite them.

As their friends meandered off in different directions, Skip flagged down his mother, Aunt Rose, and Anita. "Cassandra and I are going to head over to the ice cream shop. Would you like to meet us there for dessert?"

Before the ladies could reply, Skip's little sisters started jumping and screaming. "Yeah!"

Erin smiled at him. "Skip, you're not spending the money that the church just gave you. Are you?"

"I can't. The pastor gave me a check, and you know I haven't been to the bank, yet. I have the cash that Cassandra and I never had a chance to spend on our honeymoon."

While their nearest and dearest headed out the door to meet them at the ice cream shop, Skip and Cassandra found it difficult to escape their warm and caring church family who hailed them from across the auditorium and flagged them down in the foyer. People who hadn't been able to attend their wedding offered belated congratulations, hugs, and handshakes. Close friends just wanted to welcome them home. In short, practically everyone there wanted to talk to them. When they finally got out the door, someone stopped them at their car.

By the time they reached the ice cream shop, Skip expected that everyone was a good halfway through their ice cream by now. But no one had gone inside. They'd all waited in their cars for him and Cassandra to arrive.

The people at the ice cream shop were overwhelmed when Skip's small army filed through the door. The shop held six small round tables that seated four people at each. Stephanie, Sandy, and Suzi all sat at one table licking ice cream cones. Three-year-old Scooter sat with Rose and Erin eating her cone while the ladies chatted over their sundaes. The last to order, Skip paid the bill, picked up his chicken strip basket, and joined Cassandra and her family.

Melanie's eyes widened. "You're not having ice cream?"

"No. I'm hungry. If you'll excuse me ..." Skip bowed his head and silently thanked the Lord for his food.

The ladies sat respectfully quiet while he prayed.

Before Skip even took his first bite, he looked at Anita and said, "I was quite surprised to see you and Melanie at church this evening."

"I knew you would be," responded Anita. "And I could hardly wait to tell you."

"Tell me what?"

"While you and Cassandra were gone, Melanie and I accepted the Lord as our Savior."

"You did what?" cried Skip. "When was this? I want to know what brought you to Christ. Who led you to the Lord?"

"Your mother." Anita bit into her waffle cone. "After you and Cassandra left on your honeymoon, I called your mother. I couldn't get the image of you out of my mind the night the police spent almost five hours looking for you and finally brought you home soaking wet because they found you tied up in a ravine full of water during a horrendous thunderstorm."

"Yeah, that was a bad night for me. It's only by the grace of God I survived that at all."

"You almost died. We came very close to burying you before your wedding. And no matter how I tried, I couldn't put that thought out of my mind. So I called your mom, and she came right over. She told me that as much as she worries about you, she knew that you were in the hands of the Lord. And if He took you to be with Him, she would see both you and your dad again."

"I really look forward to seeing my dad again, but I'm not quite ready to go yet."

Anita smiled. "Well, I didn't have that assurance. Then your mom told me that Cassandra knew the Lord and asked me if I knew that I would see her again in Heaven? And I didn't. But I wanted to. So your mom shared the gospel with Melanie and me, and we both asked Jesus into our hearts and lives."

Skip wiped his tear-filled eyes. His mind whisked him back to the horrors of that night – hypothermic from sitting in freezing cold rain water up to his chest ... his hands tied behind his back ... congested with tape over his mouth ... for hours! He almost drowned. And no one knew where he was but God. Yet good came of the situation that he found himself in. Cassandra's mom and sister got saved as a result of his brush with death.

Anita changed the subject. "So tell me where you took Cassandra on your honeymoon."

Skip popped his last French fry into his mouth. "Nowhere, really."

"Nowhere!" gasped Melanie. "Come on, Skip. You left on Saturday and got back yesterday. You were someplace for three days."

Oh, no. Cassandra took a bite of her sundae and glanced at Skip, hoping to catch his eye. He was sharp, so if he caught her look, he'd pick up on her hint and change the subject. If only she had remembered to tell him not to mention their three-day stay at Uncle Woody's ranch to her mother or sister.

Skip sipped his soda. "Yeah, we were someplace. We went to see Woody and Mabel McKenzie. They have a really nice ranch."

Melanie's eyes widened. "You went to see our aunt and uncle and didn't even tell me. Aw, Cassandra."

Cassandra cringed and glanced at her mother, expecting to see angry disapproval in her eyes.

Finishing her last bite of waffle cone, Anita wiped her mouth and hands on a napkin. "That's wonderful. How are Uncle Woody and Aunt Mabel doing?"

"They're doing really well, Mom. They were thrilled to see me and to meet Skip. You're not mad that we went to see them?"

"No, Cassandra. Since Jesus became my Savior, I look at so many things differently. It was wrong of me to sever our relationship with Dad's side of the family because of what your father did. Your father's brother and his wife are two of the finest people I've ever met."

"Did you know that they're Christians, Mom?"

"Yes. And it's probably because of their prayers that we're now Christians."

Rose couldn't believe that she was sitting in an ice cream shop with Stephen's family, who were all so full of love, compassion, faith, and the joy of the Lord. Her brother's godly wife and obedient children were a tremendous testimony to his personal relationship with the Lord. How she wished that her boys could benefit from Stephen's godly wisdom and knowledge as did his own children. But, alas, she'd wasted the years she'd had to nurse a grudge which ultimately kept her sons from his godly influence.

Rose gazed at her uniformed nephew, who sat at the next table talking to Cassandra's mom. "Erin, why didn't you tell me that Skip is on the police force?"

"The subject never came up." Erin took a bite of her ice cream. "And you met Skip before you met me. Since he'd already told you about his father's death and his little sisters, it made sense to me that you'd talked about other things, as well."

"Hmm." Rose studied Skip, deep in thought, "I wonder if he could get through to Trevor and Robby for me." She was talking more to herself than Erin.

"Too close in age. His uniform would drive a wedge between them before he even had a chance to introduce himself."

Rose sighed. "But that was the very reason I came to see Stephen."

"Stephen would have been different. They would have respected his position as a law enforcement officer because of his age and probably would have been drawn to him because of his caring fatherly manner. But they'll view Skip as a meddling brother. As a result of his interference, the authority of his police uniform would drive a wedge between them as cousins and cause further rebellion, possibly getting them in trouble with the law."

With pursed lips, Rose shook her head. "Then, what should I do, Erin? I have never felt this helpless."

Erin reached across the small table and grasped her hand. "Pray for them, Rose. No matter where they go, they can't escape the Lord any more than Jonah did. God can reach them before it's too late."

Chapter 11

Skip's Proposition

By the time Skip and Cassandra started the drive home, it was almost ten o'clock, and Skip was beyond tired. Cassandra chattered nonstop. Skip didn't mind. It was an indication that she missed him.

"Did you study your driver's manual today?" he asked.

"No. I've been incredibly busy today."

Skip glanced at her. "Really? Doing what?"

"Moving in. Unboxing my clothes. Rearranging your room. Making it look pretty. Oh, Skip, you should see your room. I hope you don't mind that I moved some of your baseball stuff."

"No, I don't mind. That's not my room anymore."

Cassandra paused. "It's not? You mean, I spent all day redecorating someone else's room?"

Skip laughed. "Yes. It's your room now."

"Mine! But where are you gonna sleep?"

Skip laughed so hard, he almost couldn't get his answer out. "With you. The only time I'm ever in that room is when I'm sleeping. So I'm glad that you arranged things to your liking. 'Cause with me at work, I know that you'll spend far more time in that room than I ever did."

"Aunt Rose told me you wouldn't mind."

"Did she help you?"

"Oh, yeah. I couldn't have gotten all that done by myself. Your mom helped too. And so did Stephanie and Sandy. You know, Skip. I was so upset at the thought of having to live with your family. But I think I'm going to like it, especially having company when you're at work."

Skip followed his mother's van into the driveway. The garage door went up and Erin pulled into the two-car garage while Skip parked in the driveway next to his Aunt Rose's rental car. Piling out of the vehicles, everyone entered the house through the garage door. The last one in, Skip closed the garage door.

Cassandra grasped his hand and escorted him up the stairs to their bedroom. "Well?" she cried. "What do you think?"

"Wow! It looks so different. You really were busy today."

"So what do you think of the curtains?" asked Cassandra.

"Do you like them?" asked Skip.

"I absolutely love them."

"Then that's all that matters."

Skip looked around for his dresser. "Did you rearrange my drawers?"

"Nope, just the dressers. Everything in the dresser drawers is exactly where you left them."

"Okay, good. I need to shower and get to bed. Five o'clock comes awfully early."

The next day, despite running from one radio call to the next, Skip and Jesse squeezed in a twenty minute lunch at Becky's Beacon, where they hurriedly mapped out their baseball strategy. Checking their calendars, they selected the day, time, and location for tryouts. Then they made a list of the equipment they would need to pull together or purchase. Lastly, they divided the list of kids between the two of them so they could contact all the boys that evening.

Ordering something to go, Skip grabbed a quick burger and iced tea, devouring them before he'd even turned out of the parking lot. But instead of going back in service, he detoured to the office of his insurance agent, where he quickly added Cassandra to his car insurance policy. Within five minutes, he was back on the road. The instant he radioed dispatch his availability, they sent him on a call.

As his day progressed, so did the amount of paperwork he'd have waiting for him at the station. His day would be long enough without staying late to do paperwork. Therefore, he returned to the station thirty minutes early and finished his reports shortly after six.

With his duty day finally over, Skip didn't even take time to change clothes as he headed out the back door of the police station. He was ready to go home three hours ago but he had a stop to make on his way home. Turning out of the station parking lot, Skip headed to Mrs. Burke's house, arriving ten minutes later.

There were two cars parked at the curb in front of her house, a little white Datsun and a red Toyota Corolla. Parking at the curb behind the Toyota, Skip strolled up the front walk to her house and rapped on the door. A short, stocky woman, with coal-black hair and bloodshot eyes swung open the front door. She drew in a sharp breath and recoiled when she saw his uniform.

"What do you want?" she demanded through the closed screen door.

"Are you Leila Burke?"

"Yes."

"May I speak with your son?"

"What did he do now?"

"I take it he's been in trouble with the law before. Please get him for me. I'd like to ask him some questions," said Skip.

"Are you arresting him?"

"Not right now. I just want to talk to him. Now go get him."

"Oh, all right. Wait here." Leaving the front door standing wide open, Mrs. Burke turned and shuffled toward the stairs. "Damon! Get down here!"

"Aw, Mom! What is it now?" Damon stomped down the stairs.

Mrs. Burke pointed toward the front door. "He wants to talk to you."

"Who?" Stepping onto the hardwood floor, Damon pivoted toward the front door but jerked to a stop when he saw Skip. His round face, once flush with anger over the disturbance, suddenly paled.

After rattling the screen door with his knuckles, Skip pulled open the door and stepped into the house. "May I come in?"

With a sigh, Leila nodded. "What did he do this time?" Looking away, she motioned toward her son.

"Nothing serious. I actually dropped by to ask a favor."

"A favor?" Shock crossed Leila's face, and she glanced up at Damon in surprise.

A mask of indifference smothered Damon's look of fear. "Why me?"

"Another police officer started a project with some of the youth in this area, but he can't finish it. While attempting to pull over a little white Datsun that was racing through town, he was broadsided by a pickup truck and landed in the hospital."

Damon's color drained completely.

"Really? Damon has a little white Datsun." Mrs. Burke eyed her son suspiciously.

Skip studied Damon, contemplating his role in the botched kidnapping attempt. "What a coincidence. Is it registered in his name?"

"No, it's registered in my name because his credit isn't good enough to get a car loan."

Damon cringed. Skip certainly had enough to arrest the boy, but it was mostly misdemeanor stuff, except for that attempted kidnapping. Even then, he had only used a toy gun. Likely, he would be back on the street in a day or two at the most, and Skip wanted a more permanent solution to cure the boy's mischievous streak before he got himself into some real trouble.

Skip looked at Mrs. Burke. "I'd like Damon to help me complete the project that the other officer initiated. We're organizing a baseball team for some boys who can't seem to stay out of trouble. Hopefully, it'll get them off the streets and give them a constructive outlet."

Leila's face brightened. "I think that's a wonderful idea. Of course, he can help you."

Skip turned to Damon. "How about it, Damon? I sure could use your help."

Damon gazed down at the floor and shifted his weight from one foot to the other. "Well, um, I have a part-time job."

"I'm glad to hear that, but this won't interfere with your job."

Damon glanced at his mother, whose enthusiastic nod displayed that she wholeheartedly supported Skip in this endeavor. That seemed to put Damon on the spot, which obviously made him incredibly uncomfortable. If he refused, his mother would want to know why, and Skip knew that he didn't want her to know what he'd been involved in lately. That would force him to agree unwillingly, and Skip knew it.

With a look of defeat, Damon nodded.

"Great! Let's talk outside for a minute." Skip turned to Leila and held out his hand. "It was nice to meet you, Mrs. Burke."

With a big smile, Leila grasped his hand. "Indeed. You come back and see us again now."

"Thank you, ma'am." Skip motioned for Damon to follow him and started out the door.

Damon trailed him onto the front porch and shut the door behind them. "That was unfair! You had no right to do that to me."

"Unfortunately for you, you're one of those boys who can't seem to stay out of trouble. Would you prefer jail?"

Damon glared at him. "All right! So you got me over a barrel."

"Don't blame me. You've gotten yourself into this mess. I'm only offering you a constructive way out."

"Now what, Mr. Big Shot?"

"I want the names of your other two friends."

Damon gasped. "I can't tell you that. We have a pact among the three of us."

"Well, you and I don't have a pact between us. So I'll let your mother know that you're going to jail." Skip raised his hand to knock on the door again.

"No, don't." Leaping backward like he was about to bolt, Damon threw up both hands in surrender. "Their names are Trevor and Robby."

"Trevor and Robby what?"

Damon shrugged. "I don't know. I never asked them their last names. I only know that they're brothers, and they came here from California."

He knew more than that. And now that Skip had him talking, he would glean as much information as he could from Damon. When Skip finally left, he knew when and where Damon had met them, how long he'd known them, when they first arrived in Forest Valley, and where they were staying.

"Thanks, Damon." Pulling his notebook and pen from his shirt pocket, Skip jotted down the information about the team's first get-together. "I'll see you at tryouts. Don't be late, and stay out of trouble."

Damon sighed. "Stay out of trouble," he echoed. "Yeah, sure. Why does it sound so easy when it's so hard to do?"

Chapter 12

A Truth Uncovered

It was past seven o'clock by the time Skip walked through the front door. Cassandra flew into his arms and planted her lips against his. She felt good in his arms and Skip had no desire to let her go. He hadn't seen her all day. But he wanted to follow up with the information he'd extracted from Damon, and he still had a half dozen phone calls to make about baseball tryouts.

After a long, sweet kiss, Cassandra finally looked up at him. "Are you hungry? It'll only take a few minutes to warm your supper."

"I'm starved." Skip released Cassandra and followed her into the kitchen. He sat down at the dining room table while she warmed his supper. "Cassandra, I know we haven't seen each other much since we returned from our honeymoon, if you could call it that, but after I eat I need to run out again."

"Can I come with you?"

Skip shook his head. "No, it might be better if you didn't."

Handing Skip his plate, Cassandra sat down to visit with him while he ate. Skip bowed his head and prayed before he started eating.

"Aw, Skip, I've really missed you today. Why can't I go with you?"

"I'm sorry, Cassie. This is police work." Skip shoveled in his last mouthful and guzzled his iced tea. Depositing his empty glass and plate in the kitchen sink, he left the kitchen and bounded up the stairs into their bedroom.

Cassandra followed him. Skip changed into khaki dress slacks and a short sleeve plaid shirt. "I shouldn't be gone too long this evening, and when I get back I have to make some phone calls. But if you'd like, you can make those calls while I'm gone."

"What kind of phone calls?"

Sitting on the bed, Skip motioned for Cassandra to sit beside him. Cassandra looped her arm through his and snuggled up to him while he explained the baseball project that he had inherited from Johnny.

"So you want me to call all the kids to tell them when and where you're holding tryouts?"

"I'd appreciate it if you would. You're only calling half the list. Jesse's calling the other half. If you would do that, when I get home, the rest of the evening will be ours." Skip handed Cassandra the list of boys that needed contacting, along with the information for tryouts that she needed to pass along. "Thanks, Cassie."

Holding hands, they left the bedroom and slowly descended the stairs together. Pausing at the front door, Skip kissed her again.

"I'll be back as soon as I can." He pushed through the front door and jumped into the car, heading back to the ally where Trevor and Robby lived.

Cassandra watched through the glass door until the car was out of sight.

Coming alongside her, Erin slid an arm around her. "It's not easy being married to a police officer."

"I don't understand it." Cassandra blinked back tears. "He had more time for me when we were dating."

"Did he? You only saw him twice a week. And because of their short-handedness at the station, Skip's pulling more hours this week. But I think he's up to something tonight. His father used to do the same thing – take off right after he ate."

"Did you ever find out what he was doing?"

Erin nodded. "Eventually. He was getting kids out of trouble."

With a sigh, Cassandra said, "I think I'll go study my driver's manual some more."

The Surprise Family Union

Pulling up to the curb at the corner of a downtown street lined with stores and businesses, Skip parked his car. At this hour of the evening, most of the businesses were getting ready to close for the day, so traffic was light and the street fairly quiet.

Locking his car, Skip stepped onto the sidewalk and strolled around the corner to the alley located directly behind the businesses on the main road. This was where he had sat in his police car jotting down the license number to Mrs. Burke's Datsun.

As dusk settled over town, Skip's dark glasses intensified the dimness that surrounded him. Striding down the alley surveying the area as he walked, Skip passed by two small stairwells that led down to the doors of underground rooms. There was an alphabet letter on each door. Reaching the third small stairwell, he trotted down the six steps to a dirty white door marked with the letter "c" and knocked. When no one answered, he tried the doorknob. The door creaked as Skip pushed it open.

"Hello?"

Skip stepped inside and removed his dark glasses, sliding them into his shirt pocket. Leaving the door open to provide him with as much light as possible, he strolled through the sleeping quarters of Damon's two comrades.

A musty odor hung heavily in the air of the dark and dusty underground room. The room was dirty, covered with cobwebs, although someone had recently attempted to do some cleaning since the floor was fairly clean.

Stooping down, Skip examined the two sleeping bags on the concrete floor. They were brand new, expensive ones.

I wonder if these were stolen.

Sitting beside one of the sleeping bags was a sturdy flashlight. Skip picked it up and turned it on, creating a soft glow that illuminated the room with a dim beam of light. The batteries were dying.

Rising, he shined it around the room. It was a storage room, filled with boxes and shelves of miscellaneous items, likely for one of the businesses that were on the main road.

I wonder if they're aware that a couple of vagrants have made themselves at home in their storage room.

Then he examined everything that wasn't dusty, which indicated that it had moved in with the current occupants. Skip picked up a small Bible and opened the front cover, hoping to learn the boys' last name. A small photograph fell out. Shining the light on it, he picked it up and gazed at the picture in disbelief. This was obviously a family photo and there was his Aunt Rose. Trevor and Robby Thompson were his cousins.

Skip studied the wallet-sized photo. "I wonder why my Aunt Rose never mentioned her sons." With care, he tucked the picture into the front cover of the Bible and returned the Bible to its original location.

Skip stood. Switching off the flashlight, he set it down where he had found it.

"I think I'll drop in again tomorrow."

Closing the door behind him, he skipped up the steps two at a time and trotted back to the car. He was going home to see his wife.

Cassandra peeked out the window for the third time in less than a minute. *Where's Skip? He said he wouldn't be gone long, but it's almost dark outside.*

A month shy of her fourth birthday, Scooter trotted down the stairs with a big story book under her arm. "C'sandwa, you read to me?"

"Aren't you supposed to be in bed? You're not even in your pajamas yet." Cassandra took the book from her little sister-in-law. "You go get in your jammies. Then we'll read."

Scooter scrambled up the stairs. She had just disappeared from view when Cassandra felt something poke her in the back.

"All right, lady, you're under arrest. Don't try anything funny, or I'll have to kiss you."

With a big grin, Cassandra tossed the book onto the sofa and threw up her hands. She would try something funny all right, and Skip was about to end up on the floor.

"Cassie, aren't you going to try something so I can kiss you?" asked Skip in bewilderment.

Quick as lightning, Cassandra spun around and seized his arm. Swinging her leg behind his, she shoved him. Skip lost his balance and tumbled to the carpeted floor.

Unable to resist, Cassandra started tickling him. Skip's laughter brought his four young sisters racing into the living room. Seeing him down, they jumped on him.

Skip struggled to escape their torture. "Mom! Help!" He laughed so hard he could barely get the words out. "Cassandra, stop!"

Cassandra giggled at him. "Why?"

"What's going on in here?"

Erin and Rose dashed into the living room. Erin laughed and returned to the kitchen, but Rose clapped her hands.

"Who wants a cookie?"

The girls leaped up and raced into the kitchen. Skip lay on the floor breathing hard.

Kneeling beside him, Cassandra fingered his blond hair. "Oh, you poor thing. I tickled the breath right out of you."

"But I'm recovering quickly because I heard Aunt Rose say there are cookies in the kitchen." Skip sat up and drew in a slow, deep breath. "Aah, and they're homemade. Let's go grab a couple before they're all gone."

Rising to his feet, Skip helped Cassandra up. Then he led the way into the kitchen. His little sisters sat around the dining room table with cookies and milk while his mother and Aunt Rose stood near the sink talking softly. The freshly baked chocolate chip cookies sat unguarded on the kitchen counter cooling.

Skip scooped up a handful and hurried Cassandra from the kitchen. Opening the front door, he headed outside into the cool night air.

Cassandra followed him, closing the door behind her. "Where are we going?"

Skip handed her three cookies. "Let's go for a walk. It's such a pretty evening, and I haven't seen you all day."

Munching on his cookies, Skip strolled down the sidewalk toward the nearby park.

"A walk?" said Cassandra. "But it's almost dark out."

"This is a safe neighborhood." Skip finished his cookies and grasped Cassandra's hand.

When they reached the park, Cassandra pulled him toward the swings. "Will you push me?" She plunked into the swing and kicked herself back.

Skip strolled up behind her and gave her a push. "Did you make those calls for me?"

"Yes. You have a very difficult team. Those boys were not receptive."

"I didn't think they would be. Did you have a chance to study your driver's manual today?"

"Oh, yeah, I studied it for quite awhile. A lot of it I already knew, so I think I'm about ready to test."

Skip gave her another push. "Well, as soon as I'm able, I'll take you to WyDot to take the test."

"Thanks, Skip." As she gently pumped, Cassandra gazed up at the night sky. "It's a beautiful night. There must be a zillion stars out."

"Yeah." Skip looked up at the stars. He loved the vastness of space. It reminded him that he served an incredibly big God, but as his mind lingered on the Creator of the universe, the sound of tiny voices interrupted his thoughts. Stepping away from the swing, he stopped pushing Cassandra and glanced around, trying to localize the sound.

"What's the matter?" asked Cassandra.

"I hear some little kids."

"Outside at this late hour?"

"Apparently. Let's go check it out," said Skip.

Cassandra hopped off the swing and grasped his hand. Together they hiked across the park toward the voices of the little ones. The two security lights strategically located at opposite ends of the park cast shadows of the playground equipment and two young children with three adult-like figures. It appeared as if they were simply tormenting the youngsters.

Not certain if the children were in any immediate danger, yet knowing that they should have been home long ago, Skip released Cassandra's hand and raced to their aid.

As he drew near, he recognized the children. They were the seven-year-old Carson twins – Aaron and Abbie. And to his dismay, he also recognized the boys who were harassing them.

Chapter 13

Trouble at the Park

Skip put his hands on his hips. "Aw, Damon!"

The twins raced to Skip.

"Skip, make him give us back our ball," said Abbie.

"Come and get it," taunted Trevor, dribbling it like a basketball.

"Mommy wanted us home before dark," yelled Aaron. "Now gimme that ball! It's ours!" But when Aaron tried to intercept his dribble, Trevor snatched it up and fired it to Damon.

Abbie sniffled. "Please give it back. Daddy just bought it today, and he will be mad if we lose it."

"Give me the ball, Damon," said Skip.

Damon shuffled backward with the ball as if he expected Skip to walk over to him and snatch it out of his hands, but Skip didn't move. Damon's gaze shifted from Skip to Robby, who motioned for him to relinquish the ball. Then he looked over at Trevor, who bounced around waving his arms for Damon to toss the ball back to him.

Skip wanted to shake some sense into Damon. And the thought that the other two were actually related to him made him sick to his stomach. They had nothing better to do than tease little kids. "Does this kind of game make you boys feel like men?"

At Skip's words, shock crossed Robby's face. Shaking his head, he turned around and walked away.

Glancing one last time at Trevor, Damon finally shrugged and tossed the ball to Skip. "I ... I'm sorry." Spinning around, he followed Robby.

"Hey, wait for me." Trevor took off after them.

"Thanks, Skip." Abbie ran into his arms and gave him a big hug.

"Come on, I'll take you home." Handing the ball to Aaron, Skip grasped his hand while Cassandra took Abbie's hand. Together they walked the children across the park toward their house, meeting up with their worried parents before they even got out of the park.

Leaving Abbie and Aaron with their parents, Skip took Cassandra's hand, and they headed home. Skip yawned. The long days were catching up with him. A honking horn startled him and he jumped. Damon pulled up beside them and rolled down the window of his mother's little white Datsun.

"You guys want a lift? You look beat."

From this side of the park, it would take Skip and Cassandra twenty minutes to walk home, and Skip was anxious to get home. He needed a little relaxation. Yet he wasn't certain he trusted these boys enough to get into the car with them.

Skip studied Damon's expression. He certainly looked sincere. "So what brought you guys to this side of town? None of you live around here."

"Something to do," said Damon. "This is a nice park."

"Indeed, it is, but can't you find something to do besides bully little kids?"

Damon sighed. "I suppose we could."

"Good. Why don't you try? I'll see you tomorrow." Skip knocked on the car door and backed out of the street.

Damon wasn't sure what prompted him to offer Skip and his girlfriend a ride, but it disappointed him that they didn't accept. He liked the thought of having the upper hand, especially over that troublesome cop who thwarted their attempt to grab his girlfriend the other day and then showed up at his door making demands. If they'd gotten into his car, Damon would have had the advantage this time, especially with Trevor along. He wasn't so sure about Robby. But he and Trevor always had a good time together. They could have stranded that cop somewhere and taken off with his pretty girlfriend.

Trevor interrupted his thoughts. "Damon, are you sure he's a cop?"

"I have no doubt. He showed up at my house today in uniform."

"You didn't tell him where we live, did you?"

Skip already knew they were sleeping in one of those basement storage rooms in that back ally. He would have located them regardless of the information that Damon supplied him, so he saw no reason to tell Trevor that Skip had squeezed the letter on the door out of him. "Nope."

"Good. I'm starting to think it was a bad idea for us to come here to visit our Uncle Stephen."

"I don't get it," said Robby. "He invited us, yet we can't locate him. And there's a reason that Mom hasn't talked to him in twenty years."

"I can't believe that there's not one Shaughnessy listed in the phone book," said Damon.

"Hey, Damon, what's the name of that cop?" asked Trevor.

"Skip."

"Skip what?"

Damon shrugged. "I don't know. I was so rattled when he came to see me today that I never looked at his name plate."

"Hmm." Trevor rubbed his chin. "He probably doesn't know our uncle anyway. He can't be any older than I am, and our uncle is likely retired from the police force by now."

Robby sighed. "Trevor, I'm tired of this ghost chase. We left Los Angeles almost two weeks ago, and we're no closer to finding our Uncle Stephen than we were when we arrived. Don't you have his address?"

"Um, I seem to have misplaced it. But aren't we having loads of fun? Isn't it great to be free? What if we find our uncle and he's worse than Mom?"

"Worse than Mom in what way? At home, we lived in a nice clean house and had plenty to eat. I hate living in that dirty rat hole on the scraps that you steal."

"That's all we can afford on my income," said Trevor.

"You don't have an income. You don't even have a job."

"And I like it that way. If you don't, you're free to run home to Mom."

"I don't have any way to get home. You know that."

"Aw, now that's just too bad," said Trevor.

Holding hands while swinging their arms, Skip and Cassandra hiked home.

As they neared the house, Cassandra said, "Skip, you look awfully tired. Why didn't you accept a lift home, so we didn't have to walk? You obviously knew the driver."

"Cassandra, I know it's kind of dark out, but didn't you recognize any of those boys? Those were the boys who tried to kidnap you with toy guns, and they were all three in the car."

Cassandra gasped. "That was them? I won't make that mistake again. Tonight I got a good look at them all. I can't believe they had the audacity to offer us a ride."

Skip laughed. "Maybe they were hoping to finish the job. They might very well have stranded me out in the middle of nowhere and taken off with you in the car."

"I don't think that's funny."

Her alarm at the mere thought of it made him laugh even harder.

"Skip!"

Skip was so tired, he couldn't stop laughing. He found the whole situation amusing, and the more upset Cassandra got, the funnier it seemed.

Jerking her hand out of his, Cassandra turned her back to him.

Still laughing, Skip took her arms and turned her around to face him. "Now do you regret marrying me?"

Cassandra giggled and kissed him. "Not yet, but if you keep laughing at me, I will."

"I'm not laughing at you. I'm just tired." Skip kissed her again. "And I think it's funny that they tried it again. Even if they were really going to take us home, I don't want them to know where we live. Do you? They're unpredictable, and we don't need them showing up at our house for any reason." Sliding his arm around her, Skip escorted her into the house.

Skip's alarm sounded at five o'clock and he rolled out of bed, rubbing the sleep from his eyes. Today was Friday, which meant that tomorrow was baseball tryouts.

Ugh. As much as he loved baseball, he was not looking forward to the aggravation he'd be forced to deal with while trying to coach those boys. Too bad Johnny was still in the hospital. Those kids would respond to his direction a lot quicker, and he might get them to cooperate with Skip. As it was, Skip didn't know if they would listen to him or Jesse at all.

He tossed things over in his mind while he got ready for work. Slipping quietly down the stairs, Skip dropped to his knees beside the sofa.

He prayed every morning before leaving the house, asking God to protect him at work, to give him safety on the road, and to give him the wisdom needed in dealing with the situations that he encountered today. As he prayed for other pressing issues and for his family, he felt impressed to pray especially for Scooter. He hoped she wasn't coming down sick. Finally, he prayed about tryouts, his cousins, and Damon. Those boys didn't realize it, but they were headed for some serious trouble.

Rising to his feet, Skip snatched up his car keys and headed out the door. "Lord, help me to get hold of Trevor and Robby today. I want them and Damon at tryouts tomorrow."

Chapter 14

Trouble at the Pool

Up by seven, Cassandra hurriedly dressed, made the bed, spent time with the Lord in prayer, and read God's word. Then she reviewed her driver's manual again.

"I think I'm ready to test, Lord. But if I wait for Skip to take me, it might be the middle of July."

Ask Erin. The thought was so clear, she glanced around the room.

Ask Erin? thought Cassandra. *Sure, why not? The worst she can say is no.*

Laying her driver's manual on the dresser, Cassandra trotted down the stairs and into the kitchen, where Erin and Rose were visiting over a cup of coffee.

"Good morning, sleepy head." Erin poured her a cup of coffee.

"Thanks," said Cassandra. "Hey, Erin, I have a really big favor to ask. Would you be able to take me to

WyDOT this morning so I can test for my temporary license?"

Erin and Rose exchanged glances, and they both nodded.

"Maybe we can work an exchange," said Erin. "It's supposed to be a really hot day, and you would be a tremendous help to us if you would take the girls swimming this afternoon. That would keep them busy while Rose and I run to the store."

Rose nodded. "We have a birthday party to plan."

Cassandra gasped. "Oh, my gosh. Skip's birthday. I'd love to take them swimming, Erin. I'll invite Melanie to join us. She'll love it. And I'll have help keeping an eye on them."

"Thanks, Cassandra. They shouldn't be difficult to watch. Scooter is the only one who can't swim, and there is a lifeguard at the pool. We really appreciate this."

By the time Cassandra was ready to go to WyDot, all the girls were up.

"Can we go? Can we go?" cried the two youngest.

"I want to go, too," said Sandy. "I'll get dressed right now."

"*Whoa.*" Erin grabbed her arm to keep her from dashing off. "I need all of you to stay home to take care of Aunt Rose. She won't know what to do if no one's here."

"She can come, too," said Stephanie.

"Oh, no," said Rose. "I don't want to go. Your mom and Cassandra are going someplace where no one's allowed to talk or run or play. Cassandra's going to take a test so she can get her learner's permit so she can learn to drive like Skip does. So everyone that goes inside has to be real quiet. They can't talk or play."

"Or whisper?" asked Suzi.

Rose shook her head. "No talking at all, not even in a whisper. Why don't you girls stay home with me and we'll eat breakfast."

The girls all looked at each other.

"I think I'll stay home with Aunt Rose," said Stephanie.

"Me, too," agreed Sandy.

That settled it. Now, nobody wanted to go. Even Erin, but she'd promised Cassandra. So they headed out the door before the girls changed their minds about going.

The day had heated up so quickly that by eleven o'clock, it was already 90 degrees outside. Cassandra knew that the temperature could easily reach 95 degrees today, so she gladly invited Melanie over to go swimming with her and the girls. The community swimming pool was a mere five minute walk from the house.

While Cassandra and Melanie prepared an early lunch for the little ones, Rose and Erin quietly slipped out the door to go shopping.

Keeping the girls preoccupied, Cassandra hustled them to the dining room for lunch. Then while she and Stephanie cleaned up the kitchen, Melanie helped the younger three get ready to go swimming. Cassandra didn't want them to notice their mom had disappeared.

Wiping off the table, Stephanie said, "Hey, Cassie, where did Mom and Aunt Rose go?"

"They just had a little running to do. And your mom thought you'd enjoy going swimming more than sitting in a hot car."

"We're going swimming? Oh, boy." She tossed the cloth onto the kitchen counter and ran up the stairs to get ready to go.

With a grin, Cassandra trotted up the stairs and into her room to get herself ready.

Since Erin didn't approve of her daughters walking down the sidewalk in their bathing suits, the girls all pulled on tee shirts and shorts over their swimwear. Cassandra and Melanie already had summer clothes over their swimsuits. Slipping into flip flops, the girls gathered their towels. Scooter grabbed her bucket of water toys, and the girls followed Cassandra and Melanie out the door.

Robby was homesick. He missed his mom. He missed his friends. He missed sleeping in a comfortable bed, taking a hot shower, and eating a good meal. He was miserable here. He wanted to go home. All Trevor wanted to do was to have fun at someone else's expense. Robby enjoyed having fun, too, but he found no enjoyment in the trouble that Trevor brought to others.

He wished he'd never allowed his brother to talk him into coming to Wyoming.

With a heavy sigh, he glanced over at Trevor and Damon, who were off by themselves, probably cooking up another scheme. Only this one might get them all thrown in jail.

"Hey, Robby, come on," called Trevor. "Let's go have some fun. But we gotta run home and change first."

I knew it, thought Robby. *They're up to no good again. Well, this time I'm not going. They can go without me.*

"It's a really hot day, and Damon knows where we can go swimming."

Robby's eyes widened. "Swimming?" That did sound like fun.

"He said there's a community swimming pool down the street from the park we were at last night, and he'll drop us off there before he goes into work. So let's run home and change into our trunks."

"Damon can't go?"

"Nope, he's gotta work. But he'll run us over there."

The boys dashed back to their hideout and hurriedly changed into their trunks. They didn't have towels, but it was such a hot day that they didn't think it would matter. The warm air would dry them when they were ready to come home.

Cassandra bathed the girls in sunscreen before sending them off to play. She didn't want any of them to get burned. Seven-year-old Sandy ran straight for the slide.

"Sandy, don't run!" called Cassandra. "You have to walk." She turned to Stephanie and Suzi. "That goes for you two, as well. Absolutely no running."

"We know," said Stephanie. "Sandy just got excited and forgot."

Holding Scooter's hand, Cassandra stood there for a minute, surveying the pool activity. Sandy slid down the slide into the pool, plunging under the water. Stephanie jumped off the diving board into the deep end. A moment later the girls surfaced and swam to the side. Five-year-old Suzi inched her way down the big wide steps and waded over to join Abbie Carson. Melanie dived into the pool at the deep end and swam the length of it. Everyone was already enjoying the water, except her and Scooter.

"Come on, Sweet Pea. Let's go for a swim." Releasing Scooter's hand, Cassandra sat down at the edge of the pool and slid in. Then she reached for her little sister-in-law. Scooter set down the bucket of toys, and Cassandra lifted the child into her arms. Together they waded into the cool water.

Cassandra played with Scooter in the water for about half an hour. Although she knew that Melanie was keeping an eye on the other three, she frequently glanced around to see where they were and what they were doing.

Melanie swam over to her and scooped the three year old into her arms. "Go for a swim. I'll take Scooter over to the shallow end where she left her toys so she can play."

"Thanks, Melanie." Cassandra dived under the water and swam off. When she bobbed to the surface at the other end of the swimming pool, she saw that Melanie had set Scooter on the side of the pool with her feet in the water, dipping and pouring water with her colorful little cups into her bucket.

Cassandra and Melanie took turns watching Scooter in between laps. While Melanie was swimming, Cassandra stood in the water next to Scooter. Once again she glanced around for the girls, but she gasped when two of her would-be kidnappers strolled through the gate. Although they'd only been swimming about forty-five minutes, she decided it might be a good time to gather the girls and head home. If necessary, she'd hook up the sprinkler or the slip and slide to keep the girls outside while Aunt Rose and Erin finished their birthday plans.

"Melanie." Cassandra whispered loudly, trying to get her sister's attention without drawing attention to herself.

Since Melanie was simply standing in the water looking the other way, Cassandra knew that her sister didn't hear her. Keeping an eye on Scooter, Cassandra paddled out to her sister, whispering in her ear and pointing toward the boys.

"Aw, Cassie. What are they going to do in a crowded pool area?"

"I don't know, Melanie, but those boys are trouble. They tried to kidnap me."

Melanie gasped. "You're kidding."

The girls glanced over at Scooter, who contentedly poured water from one cup to another. Suzi was still playing on the pool steps with Abbie. Sandy was in line for the slide again. But where was Stephanie? Cassandra skimmed the crowd in search of her young sister-in-law.

Her eyes widened when she saw the girl talking to the younger of the two boys. Afraid he might be up to no good, Cassandra hollered at Stephanie.

"Stephanie, get away from him." Her shout drew attention to the boys. *"Now."*

Cassandra swam to the side as fast as she could. Stephanie slowly backed away from him.

"It's them, Mommy," chimed the Carson twins.

Not sure what was happening, Robby looked to his brother for guidance. Trevor shrugged. Glancing around at all the stares they were getting, the boys slowly retreated. Robby's mouth dropped open when the girl his brother had tried to kidnap scrambled from the pool and grabbed the sweet youngster he'd just been talking to as if he were a threat to her. At the same time, the twins' father slowly approached them. Other parents grabbed their children.

Robby and Trevor bolted in opposite directions. All chaos erupted as children screamed and ran, mothers called for their children, and the lifeguard attempted to intercept Trevor.

Scurrying past some children, Robby leaped across the corner of the pool and bumped a small child into the water. But no one else seemed to notice.

Chapter 15

Caught in the Crush

Robby jerked to a stop, but his brother shouted at him. "Come on, Robby, let's get out of here before someone calls the police."

With no time to think it through, Robby simply followed his brother's orders. Leaving the youngster floundering in deep water, he raced after Trevor, but stopped right outside the gate.

Trevor grabbed his arm. "Don't stop."

"That little girl, Trevor. I knocked her into the pool."

"Who cares? Let her be somebody else's problem."

Robby twisted out of his brother's grasp and peeked inside the gate to see if anyone had even noticed that she'd fallen in. But he couldn't see past the panicked crowd of people milling about on the deck.

As a distant siren grew louder, Trevor grabbed his arm and pulled him toward the road. "Never mind her. Let somebody else think of her. It's time to think of ourselves."

Robby couldn't believe what his brother had just said. If that child drowned because of him, how could he live with himself? "No, Trevor. I've got to go back. Nobody saw her fall in."

"Go, then," yelled Trevor. "You're on your own."

Ignoring his brother, Robby raced through the gate and dived into the pool, aiming toward the drowning child like a missile.

Cassandra had hold of Stephanie, but the people on the deck were so thick that she had lost sight of Sandy and Suzi, and she could no longer see Scooter. *Scooter!*

Caught in the crush, Cassandra frantically pushed her way through the crowd toward the pool, dragging Stephanie with her. At this point, there were more people on the deck than in the water. It was going to be difficult enough finding the other three without losing the child she had in tow.

Jostling her way through the crowd of people, Cassandra finally reached the side of the pool. Standing catty corner from where she had left the little one sitting, Cassandra's eyes darted across the water with fearful anticipation. Scooter's toys sat on the edge of the pool, but she was gone.

Scanning the crowd on the opposite side of the pool, Cassandra's intense fear melted into partial relief when she spotted Melanie. Suzi and Sandy stood on either side of her, holding her hands. But where was Scooter?

Fighting the panic that swelled up within her, Cassandra frantically glanced around. When she didn't spot the child wandering around the deck, her eyes swept over the water. Could she have fallen in? There was so much commotion that no one would notice a little three-year-old fall into the pool. As her eyes skimmed the calm pool water, a boy bobbed to the surface with a limp little girl in his arms.

"Scooter."

Cassandra attempted to jostle her way around the outside of the pool, but no one would let her through. The crowd grew thicker as everyone clustered around the rescuer to see what was happening.

Robby gently laid the child on the pool deck. Hoisting himself out of the water, he knelt beside her and tilted her head to the side, emptying her mouth of all water before he sealed his mouth over her mouth and nose. Robby gave her a couple of gentle puffs of air. Then he rolled her to her side where she spit out more water and some of her lunch. As the crowd parted for the lifeguard to get through, the child drew in a sharp breath and started to cry.

Since no one seemed to be in a rush to reach her, Robby stood and lifted her into his arms. "Shh, sweetheart, you're okay."

The lifeguard touched her back. "Is she all right?"

"I think so."

"Who does she belong to?"

"I don't know," said Robby, bouncing her gently as her crying subsided.

"You don't know her at all? I don't know who caused the panic this afternoon, but I do know that you were on your way out that gate in an awfully big hurry. And you came running back to rescue a drowning child?"

Desperate to reach Scooter, Cassandra released Stephanie and shoved her way through the crowd.

People responded in anger and irritation.

"Hey, lady, watch where you're going."

"Yeah, what's the big idea?"

Cassandra didn't care how they felt being pushed or jostled. She had to reach Scooter and make sure she was all right. Squeezing through the crowd clustered around the boy holding the little one, she heaved a sigh of relief as she finally lifted the child into her arms.

Tears streaming down her cheeks, Cassandra embraced and kissed her. Despite the trouble this boy had caused in the past, he saved Scooter from drowning, and Cassandra felt indebted to him.

"I'm so sorry," he said. "I accidentally knocked her in."

Cassandra raised an eyebrow. He knocked her in while trying to escape? Yet, he came back to save her. There was so much chaos and confusion that no one else saw her fall into the water, and Cassandra couldn't get through the clusters of people to find her. If it weren't for the courage of the very boy she considered a troublemaker, Scooter might have died.

"What's going on here?"

Cassandra looked over at Officer Tim DeShea, who slid through the crowd to reach the center of the commotion.

Someone pointed at Robby. "That boy's causing trouble."

"What's your name, son?"

"Robby Thompson, and I didn't do anything."

Tim glanced from person to person. "Who called the police? What's your complaint against this young man?"

Everyone looked around, but no one spoke.

Cassandra knew that she had inadvertently created an atmosphere of panic when she yelled across the pool deck for Stephanie to get away from Robby. And yet, the boy she considered a threat returned to save Scooter, despite the animosity against him.

"I'm sorry you were called, Tim. There's no trouble here," said Cassandra. "Just a lot of excitement. Scooter fell into the pool, and Robby saved her."

"Is she all right?" he asked. "Do I need to call for a rescue squad?"

"No. Thanks to Robby, she'll be fine."

"All right. If there's no trouble here, then I'll be going. See you later."

"Bye, Tim. If you happen to see Skip, don't mention this to him. It will worry him needlessly."

Tim nodded. "Not a word.

Robby breathed a sigh. "Thanks for not turning me in."

"Turning you in for what? Being a general nuisance or attempting to kidnap me with a toy gun? Thanks for saving Scooter."

"Y-you're welcome."

As the crowd started to dissipate, and people returned to their swimming and family activities, a middle-aged man approached them. "Young man, you're not a member of this pool. Who invited you to swim?"

Before Robby could answer, Cassandra spoke up, "He's a guest of ours. I forgot to sign him in. Sorry."

Lowering Scooter to the deck, Cassandra took her hand and escorted her over to the table located under the awning. Robby followed her. Cassandra signed him in as their guest. After signing him in, she led him and Scooter over to her sister, who had corralled Skip's little sisters into a corner so she didn't lose any of them.

"What are we doing, Cassandra?" asked Melanie. "Are we taking the girls home or what?"

"Home," chimed Stephanie and Sandy.

"No. There's been a change of plans. This is Robby. I invited him to stay and swim as our guest." Cassandra introduced each of the girls to Robby.

"You look familiar," said Stephanie. "I've seen your picture before."

"I kinda doubt that," said Robby. "I'm from California. I've only been in this town for a few weeks. It must have been someone who looked like me."

"No, it was you," insisted Stephanie. "I know your mom. And she showed me your picture a few days ago on an airplane."

"Uh-huh. Well, if you say so."

Cassandra looked from Stephanie to Robby. *Stephanie Rose Thompson. Robby's last name is also Thompson. It sure sounds like he's related. And if he's related to Aunt Rose, then he's related to us.*

Robby couldn't believe Cassandra invited him to stay as their guest after all the mischief he'd been involved in with his brother. Come to find out, Skip was her husband, not her boyfriend. Trevor irritated the fire out of him by requiring him to pull these stunts to be accepted. And he hated it. It made him feel good to rescue Scooter this afternoon.

An hour later, Cassandra took the little ones home and returned to the pool. While she was gone, Robby phoned Damon, asking his friend if he would pick him up after work. Not knowing when Damon got off, Robby had to think ahead. Damon arrived ninety minutes later, allowing him plenty of time to swim with the girls.

The moment he walked through the basement door, Trevor exploded all over him. "Why did you do that to me?"

"Do what?"

"You know perfectly well what I'm talking about, Robby. If you hadn't gone back, the police wouldn't have grabbed you."

"I had to go back, Trevor. I knocked that little girl into the pool. She would have drowned, and it would have been my fault. I didn't want to live with that on my conscience."

"Well, where have you been all this time? Were you arrested after you saved her?"

"No. The police didn't bother me. I stayed to swim."

Trevor's mouth fell open. "No way."

Robby nodded. "And I'm starved. Damon said that he'd be back in a while to get us and we'd go raid his refrigerator. His mom's going out for the evening and won't be back until about nine thirty."

"Great! I'm famished!"

Chapter 16

Hiding in the Shadows

By the time Skip left work, it was almost seven o'clock. He was pulling such long hours that he wore his uniform to and from work. But at least he was off tomorrow. His one and only day off happened to fall on a Saturday, but he suspected that Captain Kramer gave him Saturday off because of baseball tryouts. He and Jesse both had to be there, and they couldn't do it if they were on patrol.

Skip's mind wandered as he drove home. He needed to run by the hospital to see Johnny. As much as he loved baseball, he dreaded facing those incorrigible teenage boys at tryouts tomorrow. He had two wayward cousins who needed some serious redirection. He would try to catch them tonight. His young bride was waiting for him at home, and their honeymoon had gotten abruptly canceled. In addition, he'd promised to take Cassandra to get her learner's permit and teach her how to drive. Yet with these long hours, that was a promise that would have to be put on hold for the time being. Skip hated making a promise that he couldn't keep.

Skip spun his car into the driveway and wearily started up the front walk.

Cassandra met him at the door with a kiss. "All done for the day?"

"No, I only came home to grab a bite to eat. Then I have to run out again."

"Aw, Skip. Again? Where are you going this time? Will you be gone long? Can I go with you? I have something to tell you." Cassandra looped her arm through his and escorted him toward the kitchen.

Before he could answer any of her questions or ask her anything, his little sisters converged on him.

"Skip." squealed four exuberant little voices.

"Whoa."

Skip stumbled as the girls slammed into him, but Stephanie grabbed his arm and steadied him, allowing him to regain his footing and keep from falling.

The girls usually knocked him down and piled on him the moment he walked through the door. But Erin had told her daughters that under no circumstances were they allowed to knock him down when he was in uniform. He could get hurt falling on his equipment-laden police belt and if his gun accidentally discharged, someone could get killed. It pleased Skip that Stephanie remembered that.

While Cassandra warmed his supper, Skip sat down at the dining room table and the two youngest crawled up on his knees.

"We missed you, Skip," said Sandy. "What took you so long to come home?"

"I had to work late. Now it's time for me to eat, so go play."

After hugging and kissing him, the girls scampered off. Cassandra set his plate on the table in front of him. Embracing him from behind, she held him tightly while he bowed his head and prayed.

"I want to go with you," she whispered in his ear.

"It may not be safe for you. Now tomorrow, you may come with me if you'd like."

Sliding her hands up his arms, she massaged his shoulders while he ate. "How long will you be gone?"

Skip emptied his glass and set it down. "I don't know. I'm going to see a couple of guys. They may be home when I get there. But if they're not, I intend to wait for them, even if I'm there till midnight."

"Why is that dangerous?"

Shoveling in his last mouthful of food, Skip collected the dirty dishes and stood. "I don't know these guys, and I'm not sure how they'll react when they see me. So I'd better go alone this evening." He deposited his dishes in the sink and kissed Cassandra on the cheek. "Wait up for me. Okay?"

"Be careful."

The Surprise Family Union

As Skip drove across town, he yawned, contemplating what he hoped to accomplish from this visit. He wanted to see these boys turn from troublemaking to sports. It would be ideal if they volunteered to play on his team, but he suspected that he'd end up drafting them, like he did Damon.

Then it hit him. Cassandra said she had something to tell him. But she didn't tell him anything. Now it was going to bug him until he got home. Hopefully, it wasn't anything bad, like she had decided she didn't want to live there anymore.

Pulling over to the curb a little past eight, Skip stepped from his car and hit the remote lock. Then he hiked around the corner of the wide city sidewalk and into the alley directly behind the row of stores on the main street.

By the time he reached the door to his cousins' basement dwelling, it was dusk. He was tired and ready for bed, but this was too important to put off. These boys weren't just any troublemakers. They were related to him. How did that happen?

Skip rapped loudly, listening for any sound coming from within the dingy storage room. When no one answered his knock, he slowly pushed open the door and stepped inside.

The room was so dark that he removed his dark glasses. A shred of light filtered through a tiny window at the top of the basement wall. Quietly closing the door, he sat down on a wooden crate up against the wall to wait. Skip folded his glasses and slid them into his shirt pocket. With a yawn, he leaned back against the wall, closed his eyes, and promptly fell asleep.

Jolted awake by the sound of voices, Skip looked over at the boys entering the room. Darkness just about swallowed them up. If it weren't for one lone street lamp at the end of the ally, the room would be pitch dark. But the lamp shone through the open doorway, giving the boys a glimmer of light by which to see.

"How do you like that Damon?" yelled Trevor. "He let a stupid cop blackmail him into helping a bunch of dumb kids play baseball."

Skip sat up and listened. In the shadows, he could barely make them out. Robby followed his brother into the room and kicked the door shut just as a flashlight flickered on. The battery was weak and the light was dim, but it allowed them enough light to navigate their way to their few belongings in the center of the room.

Still sitting on the crate up against the wall, Skip was practically invisible. They might see him through the dim light if they thought to look for an intruder, but they weren't expecting someone else to be hiding in their hideout.

"It sounds fun to me," said Robby. "I wish I could play."

Trevor sprawled onto his sleeping bag and folded his hands behind his head. "Oh, Robby, don't be juvenile."

"You're calling me juvenile? You were the one teasing little kids in the park. And look at all the trouble you caused that poor store owner. And you were the one who attempted to kidnap that girl with a toy gun."

Trevor burst out laughing. "That was a good one."

"Grow up, Trevor. That was juvenile. I'm tired of living this way. I want to go home."

"Go ahead! Run home to Mom, you big baby. But I'm staying right here. I was sick of her nagging me about making good career choices, so I split."

"But why did we come all the way to Forest Valley?"

"I told you. To visit our Uncle Stephen. He sent us an invitation."

"Yeah, that's what you told me, all right. But the truth is, Mom wants us to do something good with our lives, but you just want to sponge off her wealth."

"That's not true," barked Trevor.

"Then what is true? I think we came here because Mom hated this town and you wanted to get back at her for even suggesting that we go to work somewhere."

"No."

"Yes, it is, so you might as well admit it. She has more money than we'll probably make in a lifetime, and you resent the fact that she wants us to work for a living. That's why you won't even get a job here."

Trevor clenched his fists and slowly rose to his feet. "Shut up, Robby."

"Well, you can have this old dump all to yourself. I'm done making trouble to be accepted by you. Next week,

I'm going to look for a job, and I'm going with Damon tomorrow. Maybe they'll let me play ball, too."

"Damon's only doing this because he has no choice," said Trevor.

"That may be true, but I won't be. I want to play."

"Good," said Skip. "We can use you on the team."

Chapter 17

Troublemakers Always Leave a Trail

At the sound of his voice, the Thompson boys jumped.

Snatching up the flashlight, Trevor switched it on and shined it around the room looking for their intruder. Skip could easily have dodged the slow moving light beam and remained in the darkness making his demands, but he wanted them to see him. And more importantly, for them to know that he saw them.

Sitting quietly on the crate, Skip waited patiently for the flashlight beam to reveal his presence. The instant the light beam illuminated him, the boys gasped and their mouths dropped open. Skip knew that they hadn't looked past the uniform.

"You guys need to think about what you're doing, because if your behavior doesn't change, you're headed for jail."

Skip knew that they recognized his voice because Trevor shifted the light beam to his face. Instantly blinded, Skip shielded his unprotected eyes with his hand. "Get that light out of my eyes, or I'll smash that flashlight."

Robby snatched the flashlight from his brother and redirected the beam.

Obviously too rattled by Skip's unexpected presence to fight his brother over the flashlight, Trevor stammered out a response. "H-how did you locate us?"

"Troublemakers always leave a trail."

Trevor scowled at him. "That Damon ratted on us. Didn't he?"

"Actually, when I asked him about you, he told me that he had a pact with you and couldn't give me any information."

"Then how did you find our pad?" asked Robby.

"Like I said, troublemakers always leave a trail."

"Okay, so you found us," snapped Trevor. "What do you want?"

"I came to invite you guys to play ball like I did Damon. But since Robby already wants to join the team, I only need to talk to you, Trevor."

"How do you know our names?" demanded Trevor.

"I told you, troublemakers always..."

Trevor interrupted him, "... leave a trail. Yeah, I know. But I'd like to know how that trail led you to our names."

Skip smiled. "That's a department secret. If you want the answer to that one, you'll have to join the police force."

"I don't think so. I'll just have to stay ignorant." Trevor stared at Skip's uniform. Fortunately, the room was too dark and Skip sat too far away for Trevor to read his nameplate.

"What's your name?" demanded Trevor.

Yep, that's what he was trying to do. "Skip."

"Skip what?"

Skip paused. The way that Trevor demanded information suggested that he was attempting to intimidate Skip and seize control of the situation. And Skip wasn't about to let that happen. But also, if he told them his last name, they would likely recognize it and know he was their cousin. And that was information he wasn't ready for them to have.

"My last name is not important."

"It doesn't matter, anyway," said Robby. "We just wondered if you knew anyone by the name of Stephen Shaughnessy. He's our uncle, and we're trying to locate him."

"Oh, I'm sorry," said Skip. "He died four years ago."

The news hit them like a concrete block, and the boys exchanged shocked looks. Their expressions told Skip that the thought had never crossed their minds.

Robby turned on Trevor. "You led me to believe you received an invitation from him."

"Now, what do we do?" moaned Trevor like it was nearly the end of the world.

"I'm gonna get a job," exclaimed Robby. "I'm tired of living like this."

"Good for you, Robby," said Skip. "If I can help in any way, let me know. Well, I need to get home. Tryouts are at ten thirty tomorrow morning, so I'll be here at ten o'clock to get you guys. Be ready."

Trevor displayed a tightly-clenched fist. *"Buzz off.* You may have blackmailed Damon, but it won't work on me."

"Well, you do have a choice." Slowly standing, Skip stretched his legs and snatched his handcuffs from the case on the back of his belt. He strolled over to his cousin. Seizing his arm, Skip twisted it into a joint lock behind his back and forced Trevor face first into the wall.

"Hey, what are you doing?" cried Trevor.

"You're under arrest." Skip locked him in handcuffs.

"You can't just barge in here and arrest me. What's the charge?"

"Trespassing." With a secure hold on Trevor's arm, Skip kicked his feet apart and frisked him for weapons. To his surprise, Robby shined the flashlight on his brother so Skip could see what he was doing.

"Ridiculous. I haven't been on anyone else's property without their consent."

"Oh, yes, you have. I'll bet you a dozen donuts that you don't have a lease for this place and the business owner doesn't even know you've taken up residence here. Plus, I can get you on evading a police officer, theft, attempted kidnapping, breaking and entering. I can rack up a whole list of offenses."

Trevor sighed. "All right. I'll go tomorrow. But just tomorrow."

"Wrong answer." Despite Trevor's resistance, Skip dragged him toward the door.

"Okay, okay. I'll show up for every practice and every game."

Skip paused at the door. "And you'll get a job."

"Hey! You can't force me to get a job."

"Since you're not working, you have to steal to eat. Stealing is against the law, and I will arrest you for breaking the law."

Trevor glared at Skip. "Anything else?"

"Yes. You'll stop hanging around the mall and park."

"And pool," added Robby.

"You've been causing problems at the pool, too?"

Trevor grinned sheepishly. "Hey, that wasn't my fault."

"Doesn't matter," said Skip. "Pool, too."

"Boy, you drive a hard bargain."

"Take it or go to jail. Those are my conditions, and your freedom is contingent on good behavior. You cause any more problems, and I'll lock you up so fast, you won't know what happened."

Trevor stared at his nameplate, but Skip stepped behind him and opened the door, not giving him the opportunity to realize they were cousins.

"Let's go." Skip pushed Trevor out the door.

"No, wait." Trevor stumbled and tripped over the steps leading up to the alley. "Okay. I agree to your terms."

Skip removed the handcuffs and trotted up the stairs. "Good night, gentlemen. See you tomorrow at ten. Be ready."

By the time Skip entered the house, it was almost eleven o'clock. Glancing around, he softly closed the front door and stepped into the living room. With his glasses still in his shirt pocket, he squinted at the soft glow that erupted from the small lamp sitting on the corner end table. Everything was still.

"Mom?" His mother always waited up for him. Where was she this evening? Strolling through the downstairs, Skip peeked into the kitchen. His mother was undoubtedly with Aunt Rose, but where was Cassandra? Surely she hadn't gone to bed without him.

With a sigh, Skip started up the stairs, sliding his right hand up the varnished banister. He made no attempt to hide his approach as his boots tapped the hardwood steps. Strolling down the carpeted hallway, he entered the bedrooms of his little sisters to cover them and kiss them goodnight. Then he closed their bedroom doors and headed down the hall to his own room.

Skip turned the knob and pushed open the door. Blinded by the overhead light, he slapped his right hand over his eyes.

"Skip, where are your glasses?"

"Oh, yeah, my glasses." He pulled them from his pocket and slipped them on.

Still squinting, Skip found the brightness of the overhead light almost intolerable, so he seldom used it. He preferred the soft glow of the nightstand lamp, but now that he was married, he had to consider the needs of his mate, and she certainly couldn't read by the dimness of the lamp.

Sprawled on the bed with a book, Cassandra looked up at him. She glanced up at the overhead light and back at him before scrambling off the bed. She switched on the lamp and flipped off the overhead light before diving into his arms.

"Whoa." Skip caught her, but before he could say any more, Cassandra pulled him into a tender kiss. For a moment, Skip forgot about everything but his caring wife as her sweet lips met his for a second time.

"I missed you," she whispered in his ear. With her arms still around his neck, Cassandra kissed him again. "And I have some exciting news. Guess what I did today? I tested for my learner's permit, and I passed. Your mom took me to WyDOT. Now I can drive legally."

"As long as there's a licensed driver in the car with you," added Skip. Cupping her face in his hands, he kissed her again. "I'm glad you waited up for me. Where are my mom and Aunt Rose?"

"They went shopping."

"At this hour? Mom has severe night blindness. She's not supposed to go out after dark."

"Your Aunt Rose drove."

"Oh. Guess what I learned? My Aunt Rose is wealthy. And two of the boys that tried to kidnap you with toy guns are her sons – my cousins."

Cassandra raised an eyebrow. "So Robby is related to you?"

Skip cocked his head. "Yeah. How do you know Robby?"

"He was at the pool today. And he said his name was Robby Thompson. So I wondered if he is related to your Aunt Rose."

"Well, he is. And you mustn't tell anyone, Cassandra."

"Why not?"

"I think I can turn them around, but if they find out I'm their cousin, they'll lose all respect for my authority as a police officer. They're coming to tryouts tomorrow. Whatever you do, don't give out our last name – not to anybody."

Chapter 18

Brief Encounters

The next morning, Cassandra awoke bright and early. She slid out of Skip's arms and leaned over to peek at the clock.

Seven thirty two. Time to get up.

Careful not to wake Skip, she crawled off the bed and padded softly around the room getting dressed. Sitting on the bed, she tied her shoes before reaching over to touch him. He didn't stir as she fingered his hair and caressed his smooth cheek. It amazed her that he was bordering his twentieth birthday and still didn't need to shave.

Cassandra could sit beside him all morning, but if she did, she would touch him constantly, and that would eventually wake him. He needed his sleep, so she'd better leave the room. With a contented sigh, she brushed his forehead with a soft kiss and skipped out of the bedroom, softly closing the door behind her.

It was early, so Cassandra descended the stairs quietly. She didn't want to wake the household, but when she heard the bustle of childlike activity coming from downstairs, she knew that the girls were already up. Since Erin and Rose were out so late, she suspected that they were still sleeping.

Reaching the first floor, she rounded the corner to her left and stepped into the kitchen. Cassandra jerked to a stop when she saw the ladies sitting at the dining room table fully dressed and visiting over an early morning cup of coffee.

"My, did you sleep late," said Rose. "We've been up for an hour."

"Come join us for a cup of coffee," said Erin.

Cassandra glanced around the spotlessly clean kitchen. "Have you fed the girls?"

Erin bounded to the coffee pot and poured Cassandra a cup of coffee. "Yes, dear, they ate a half hour ago." Setting Cassandra's coffee on the table with the cream and sugar, Erin rejoined Rose.

"Thank you." Cassandra pulled up a chair.

"So what are your plans for today?" asked Erin softly.

"Well, Skip's been drafted to coach a baseball team, and tryouts are at 10:30. I'm going with him. After that, I think our day is free."

"Tryouts?" echoed Rose. "Oh, that can easily take two or three hours. To be on the safe side, we'd better plan the birthday party for about four. You think you can have Skip home by four?"

"I have no idea," said Cassandra. "But I'll do my best."

"Four," gasped Erin. "We're going to feed them cake and ice cream right before dinner?"

Rose laughed. "No, silly. We're gonna order pizza. It's a party."

The excited chatter of four little girls interrupted them.

"Cassandra's up!" exclaimed Suzi.

The girls raced into the kitchen, but suddenly stopped. They all got quiet. Finally, Sandy spoke.

"Where's Skip?"

"He's still asleep, sweetheart," said Cassandra. "He's been working some long hours, and he's very tired."

She saw the disappointment wash over them as they digested this bit of information. Skip was their hero. They adored him, and Cassandra knew that they missed him tremendously while he was at work.

Scooter puckered, but Suzi smiled. "That's okay. We'll go wake him up."

"No, you won't," said Erin. "Under no circumstances are you to go into his room. You girls will all stay downstairs, and let your brother sleep. Is that understood?"

Sandy and Stephanie gave a somber nod and quietly left the kitchen.

"Did you hear me, Suzi?" demanded Erin.

Crossing her arms, Suzi frowned at her mother. "I heard you." Spinning around, she stomped out of the kitchen. Scooter ran after her.

Once the girls left the kitchen, Erin continued briefing Cassandra. "Now, I invited your mother and Melanie over. Melanie is going to take the girls to the park while we decorate for the birthday party. So if it's possible, try to delay Skip so he doesn't get here before four o'clock."

Cassandra shook her head. "That's a tall order. But I'll do my best."

Roused from a sound sleep, Skip jumped when his two youngest sisters climbed on top of him, laughing and giggling.

"Wake up, Skip," cried Suzi. "It's Saturday."

Straddling him, Suzi and Scooter bounced on him.

Lying on his side, Skip buried his head under the pillow, hoping that if he ignored them, the little ones would give up and go away. But his little sisters continued to bounce and shake him, trying to get him up.

"Skippy," said Suzi into the pillow. "It's morning."

"I know, Suzi. Please go play and let me sleep."

"We want you to get up and play with us."

"There you are." Skip heard Stephanie enter his bedroom. "Get out of his room." She crossed to his bed and lifted the youngest off of him. "You, too, Suzi. Let's go."

"I don't have to listen to you. You're not my boss."

"Mom said that we weren't to disturb him for any reason. So you get out, or *I will tell.*"

"Oh, all right." Suzi slid to the floor.

Skip's door clicked shut and his room got quiet.

"Thank you, Stephanie." Skip drifted back to sleep.

With a yawn, Skip rubbed the sleep from his eyes and looked up at the clock. Nine o'clock! He scrambled out of bed, yanked clean clothes from his dresser drawer, and dashed down the hallway and into the bathroom to shower. A short while later, he bounded down the stairs and into the kitchen looking for Cassandra.

Sitting at the kitchen table with Erin and Rose, Cassandra smiled at him the moment he walked in. "Good morning, handsome."

"Good morning, gorgeous." Skip kissed her before handing her a pen and clipboard. "You ready to go?"

"Yeah. W-what's this for?"

"I'll tell you on the way."

"What about breakfast?"

"No time. I'll meet you at the car." Without waiting for her response, Skip trotted down the basement steps and over to the clear plastic tote full of baseball equipment that he'd been gathering all week for tryouts. He hauled the box of supplies up the stairs and out to the car, depositing it into the trunk.

Leaning on Cassandra's car door, Skip talked to her through the open window. "Now that you have your learner's permit, would you like to drive?" Skip held up his keys.

Cassandra snatched the keys from him, and Skip opened her car door. Leaping from the car, she dashed around and jumped behind the wheel.

Skip slid into the car beside her. "I'll take that as a yes."

The car jerked and jolted as Cassandra struggled from first to second gear and then on to third. Driving a little too close to the solid yellow line in the center of the road, she veered across the line, so Skip reached over and grabbed the steering wheel, gently redirecting the car back into their lane of travel.

"Skip, must you do that? I don't like it when you grab the wheel."

"I don't like it when I have to grab the wheel, Cassandra. But you were straying into that guy's lane and you almost ran him off the road."

"Oh. Sorry."

"It happens. That's part of learning how to drive. But I wouldn't be a good instructor if I just let you cause an accident. Now, would I?"

Cassandra giggled. "I guess not."

With Cassandra behind the wheel, they drove a lot slower, arriving shortly after ten. Stopping the car in the alley, Cassandra released a contented sigh and looked at Skip. "How did I do?"

"Not bad." Skip leaned over and kissed her. "I'll drive now." Jumping out of the car, he hustled around to her car door and opened it for her just as the Thompson boys filed out of their basement shelter.

"You're five minutes late," snapped Trevor, climbing into the back seat of the car.

Cassandra hurried around the car and jumped into the front passenger's seat while Robby slid in beside his brother.

Skip dropped behind the wheel and snapped his seatbelt. Trevor was already being difficult. They were late because he'd let Cassandra drive, but if he never let her practice, she'd never get her license. "Sorry. It couldn't be helped."

With the tension that Trevor created, the others endured the first few minutes in silence. Finally, Cassandra spoke.

"Hi, Robby. How are you this morning?"

"I could be better. I'm kind of stiff from sleeping on that concrete floor. How's Scooter?"

"Scooter?" echoed Skip. "And just how do you know Scooter?"

Skip's mind flew through the circumstances of his recent encounters with Robby. Cassandra greeted him with more familiarity than their brief encounters warranted, especially since he never said a word to her either time. So for Robby to respond like an old friend and then inquire about his baby sister meant that they'd recently spent time together.

Chapter 19

Skip Takes Charge

Skip turned the corner, and the car got strangely quiet. It bothered him that Robby wasn't responding. "Robby?"

"Um ... I bumped into her at the pool," said Robby. "Literally. And she fell into the water. I'm really sorry. I got careless, and I didn't see her. So I just wondered how she was doing?"

"She's her usual, energetic self," said Cassandra. Turning to Skip, she continued, "Robby saved her from drowning, and I invited him to stay at the pool and swim as our guest."

"How come you didn't mention any of this yesterday?"

"Goodness, Skip, we went swimming at noon. Scooter is fine. You were in and out so fast at dinner time that it never crossed my mind to mention it. And by the time you got home last night, I was engrossed in a novel, not dwelling on the calamities of the day."

With a sigh of relief, Skip relaxed. "That makes sense."

Arriving at the ballpark, he spun the car into the parking spot next to Jesse's truck. Skip retrieved the tote of baseball equipment from the trunk of his car and passed it to Robby, directing him and Trevor to report to Jesse. Some of the boys were already there.

Snatching up the clipboard with the roster and a pen attached, he handed it to Cassandra. "Will you take role?"

"Sure, but why is it necessary?"

"Because for some of these kids, it's either this or juvenile hall. They chose to play ball, so I need a record of who's here."

"Okay." Clipboard in hand, Cassandra seated herself on the bottom bench of the bleachers.

Jesse had brought a stack of paper cups and a five-gallon cooler of ice water. By ten thirty-five the last boy arrived, so Cassandra started calling roll, marking the tiny box beside each name with a check mark.

Studying the boys for any signs of trouble, Skip didn't like the way they eyed Cassandra, so he casually strolled over to stand beside her. Once she'd finished calling names, he bent down as if to examine the list on the clipboard, but instead he whispered in her ear. "Cassie, stay near me or Jesse. Many of these boys are one step from jail, and we don't trust them."

"Where's Johnny?" demanded a tall, muscular boy. "We agreed to play for him. *Not you.*"

"He's in the hospital. And you did not agree to play for Johnny. You chose to play baseball and stay out of trouble for the next few weeks. Your alternative is Juvenile Hall. But if you've changed your mind about playing, I'll notify the authorities at Juvi to expect you this evening, and I'd be glad to call the police to transport you there."

Skip looked around at the group of belligerent boys and saw that some of the fight had already gone out of them. "So if you've changed your mind about playing ball, stand over there." Skip pointed toward a shade tree.

No one moved.

"Very well. I'm assuming by your silence that you have all decided to stay on the team. Is that correct?"

Glaring at Skip, the boys crossed their arms in defiance and gave a slight nod. It was obvious by their scorn that most of them thought they knew more about baseball than Skip. Regardless of their animosity toward him, Skip took charge. As tryouts got underway, he gave every boy an opportunity to try out for the position he desired. Then he and Jesse selected the players for each position according to their abilities.

Robby could throw the ball with incredible speed and accuracy, so they selected him as a pitcher, but Damon and Trevor refused to try out for any position.

"Skip, please don't make us play," said Damon. "We're so much older than those kids."

"Only by two years."

"Can we help you coach?" asked Trevor.

"Well." Skip pursed his lips and rubbed his chin. With Jesse's help, he didn't need another coach. He actually didn't need them here at all. He just wanted to redirect their energy and get them focused on something other than annoying people. "I don't need any more help coaching, but if you'd like to be my assistants, I know you can help in other ways."

Trevor and Damon exchanged smiles and nodded. That arrangement seemed to agree with them, which meant they would more likely help Skip than cause trouble.

Tryouts lasted for almost three hours. When they were through, Skip had Damon and Trevor pack up his equipment and deposit the tote into the trunk of his car, along with the clipboard. Then they joined the others, who had gathered around Jesse's beat up, red pickup truck drinking water.

"Same time next Saturday," said Skip. "Be here."

The boys groaned and straggled away. Climbing into his truck, Jesse waved and drove away.

Skip pulled Cassandra into his arms and kissed her cheek before whispering into her ear. "I'm starved. Let's go eat. You mind if I invite Trevor and Robby for lunch?"

Cassandra stole a peek at her watch. It was almost 1:30. She had two and a half hours to kill before going home if she hoped to have Skip home by 4:00 for his birthday party. "Not at all."

The boys were already in the back seat of the car waiting for them. Taking Cassandra's hand, Skip escorted her to the car and seated her in the front passenger's seat before jogging around the car and sliding behind the wheel.

"Are you guys hungry?" Skip cranked the engine and pulled out into traffic. "Cassandra and I are going to grab a bite to eat, and you're welcome to join us." He made eye contact with Trevor through the rear view mirror.

"You bet," said Robby. "I'm starved. I haven't had breakfast."

"You moron. You don't have any money. How are you going to pay for it?" yelled Trevor.

"I figured since Skip invited us, he was going to pay for it."

Skip flipped on his turn signal and maneuvered into the left-hand turn lane. "You're right, Robby. Since I invited you, I intended to pick up the tab."

"I don't know about Trevor, but I accept. I'm way overdue a decent meal."

Skip suspected they were both overdue. That's why he invited them to lunch. Glancing into his rear view mirror, his eyes met Trevor's again. "Trevor?"

Trevor broke eye contact. "You'd do that for me after all the trouble I've caused you?"

"Yes, unless you plan to start something at the restaurant."

Trevor dropped his head. "No. I just can't believe that you care what happens to us. You're different from anyone I've ever known."

Skip turned into the restaurant parking lot and maneuvered into a parking spot near the front door. The boys leaped out and ran toward the entrance, but they didn't go inside. They lingered outside, waiting for Skip and Cassandra.

Skip strolled around the car and opened the door for his beautiful young wife. Grasping her hand, he led the way inside.

Robby gasped. "This is a steakhouse."

"They have great food here," said Skip. "Good service, too."

The foursome ordered their food and drinks. While waiting for their lunch, Skip thought he'd get to know his cousins a little.

"So, Robby, tell me a little about yourself. What do you want to do with your life?"

"I'd love to go into professional baseball."

"That's not easy to do. You have to be better than good. You have to be exceptional."

"Boy, don't I know it. So I'm thinking of pursuing a career in computer engineering."

Skip looked at Trevor. "And what are your future plans?"

Trevor shrugged. "I don't have any."

"None? You have no idea where you're going in life?"

"Nope, and I kind of like it that way. No pressures to perform or compete. No expectations to meet. No deadlines ..."

Just then, the waitress brought their food, interrupting their conversation, and deposited everyone's plates in front of them. Skip stopped the Thompson boys from diving right into their lunch so he could ask the blessing.

"Do we have to waste time praying?" griped Trevor. "I'm starved, and my food is getting cold."

"Prayer is never a waste of time," said Skip. "Now bow your head and show respect or I'll wait until you do, and then your food will really get cold."

The boys did as Skip required, and he prayed. Then everyone started eating. For a few minutes, no one talked. They were busy filling their growling stomachs. Halfway through his steak, Skip reopened the conversation.

"So how long have you guys been in Forest Valley?"

"About three weeks." Robby gulped down his Coke and popped his last French fry into his mouth.

"That long? Did you know that your Uncle Stephen was a cop?" Skip took a bite of steak.

Trevor pushed aside his empty plate and sipped his Sprite. "Yeah, we knew."

Robby's eyes widened. "We did? I didn't."

"There's only one police station in town. Did you ask about him there?" Skip finished his last bite of steak.

With a shrug, Trevor gulped down the remainder of his Sprite. "Nope."

"Then you couldn't have been looking for him too hard."

"We weren't."

The shock on Robby's face indicated that Trevor had led him on a wild hunting expedition.

Skip glanced at Robby and back at Trevor. "Then what was your real reason for coming here if it wasn't to locate your Uncle Stephen? This is quite a distance from LA."

"How did you know we were from LA?" asked Robby.

"Damon told me."

"Oh. I thought that we were just coming for a visit."

"Think what you want," said Trevor. "You're nothing but trouble anyway. It was a mistake bringing you."

"So if you weren't really coming to see your Uncle Stephen, what brought you to Forest Valley?" Skip asked Trevor.

Trevor glared at him. "It's none of your business."

"He did it to get back at Mom," said Robby.

"Shut up and mind your own business, Robby."

"This is my business."

"Whoa." Skip threw up his hands in surrender. "I didn't mean to start a family feud."

"You didn't," said Robby. "This one started a long time ago."

"Yeah, like seventeen years ago. Hey, Skip, you want a kid brother? I'd do anything to get rid of mine."

Robby's mouth fell open.

"Trevor, somehow I doubt you mean that."

"Well, I do. He's been trouble since the day he was born. He was Dad's favorite."

"That's not true," cried Robby.

"It is true. He took you everywhere."

"That's because you wouldn't go with him. He tried to take you places, but you would never go."

Skip glanced around uneasily. As the war raged hotter between the brothers, their voices escalated, drawing attention to them from all over the restaurant.

"Shh." Skip motioned for them to lower their voices. "Everyone's looking at us."

"So let them look," yelled Trevor. "I don't care if I ever see that dumb brother of mine again. I always knew that he was Dad's favorite, but I didn't know that he was Mom's favorite until Dad died."

Crossing his arms, Robby looked away and slouched in his chair. "You're crazy. That's not true. None of it."

"Yes, it is. And the greatest thrill I've had is taking you away from Mom. She's back in LA, and you're stuck here." His face flush with anger, Trevor rose to his feet and stomped out the door.

Chapter 20

Family Friction

Erin and Rose had been busy all morning preparing for this dual surprise birthday party. The hard part was keeping the girls from figuring out what was going on. Especially Stephanie – the oldest, the smartest, and the birthday girl. If they weren't careful, she'd figure it out before the cake even came out of the oven.

So while Erin worked to prepare everything for the party, Rose took the girls out into the backyard where they could run and play. Erin had just finished frosting and decorating the cake when the doorbell rang. Without waiting to be invited in, Anita and Melanie entered the house.

It was exactly three o'clock.

"Oh, you're right on time," said Erin. "The girls are in the backyard."

"Do they know what's going on today?" asked Anita.

"No. So if Melanie can take them out the side gate, we should be good. And although the girls have been outside for a couple of hours, they will love spending an hour at the park with all the playground equipment. And that'll give us an hour to get the house decorated."

"What about Skip?"

"He's out with Cassandra. I told her to have him here by four o'clock, if it was at all possible. Hopefully, they don't get here too early."

Anita looked at Melanie. "Go get the girls. Take them out the side gate. Keep them out of the house if you can."

Melanie ran out back to get Erin's young daughters. That was the easy part. Those girls would follow Melanie anywhere. A moment later, they all filed into the house.

"Sorry, Scooter and Suzi have to use the bathroom." Melanie directed them down the hallway. "Come on girls. Let's hurry."

Stephanie paused and looked around. "Oo, what's that delicious smell?"

"Yeah, it smells good in here," said Sandy.

"Come on, Stephie," called Melanie, motioning for her to hurry. "We only have an hour."

"Only an hour? And we still have to walk to the park?" Stephanie dashed out the front door after Sandy. A moment later, the two little ones joined them.

Once the house was quiet, the three ladies went to work decorating the dining room, blowing up balloons, hanging streamers, getting out the presents and goodies.

The last thing they did was post a huge banner on the wall that said, "Happy Birthday, Skip and Stephanie."

Cassandra glanced at her wristwatch. It was 3:05. It wouldn't take them long to drop off the Thompson brothers, and they could be home in twenty minutes. How was she going to keep Skip busy for another 35 minutes? She studied Skip, considering her options.

Skip shook his head as he watched his cousin push through the double glass doors and disappear from view. Trevor had a lot of growing up to do.

Robby folded his hands on the table. "I had no idea that Trevor believed that."

"He didn't mean it."

"I'm afraid he did."

"No, he's hurt, thinking he was served a great injustice. So he retaliated in the best way he knows – with hurtful words. The best thing you can do is leave him alone for awhile to think about everything. You're welcome to stay with us."

"Skip," gasped Cassandra, barely above a whisper. "He can't stay with us because ..." Cassandra's voice trailed off.

Robby looked from Cassandra to Skip. "Maybe I should just stay with Trevor. He's already mad at me, and I don't want to get you in trouble for inviting me."

"Trust me. I won't be in trouble, and you won't be a problem. You might be sleeping on the sofa, but it's much more comfortable than a concrete floor. That'll alleviate some of your headaches and a lot of your back aches. Then next Saturday, you'll feel like playing ball. Come on, let's run Trevor home and collect your things."

Skip strolled to the cashier and paid their lunch tab. Robby and Cassandra stood near the exit, chatting softly while waiting for him. When Skip finished, he pushed through the exit door and the other two followed him to the car.

Sitting in the back seat, his arms folded tightly across his chest, Trevor stared into space. The others jumped into the car, and Skip took off. Not wanting to fuel the feud any more, no one spoke during the drive. When Skip pulled up to his cousins' basement dwelling, Trevor scrambled from the car and slammed the door.

Skip patted Cassandra's hand. "Wait here. We'll be right back."

Letting the car idle, Skip and Robby closed their car doors and trotted down the stairs into the dark room. Trevor stood with his back to them, his hands thrust deep into his pockets. Robby rolled up his sleeping bag and collected his Bible and clothes.

"You got everything?" Skip asked him.

Trevor spun around.

"I think so."

"Go wait in the car with Cassandra. I'll be right out."

Robby left the room with an armload, and Skip closed the door behind him.

"I have nothing to say to you!" yelled Trevor. "You're not my boss, and you have no right to tell me where I can go and what I can do. Now, you've come between me and my brother."

"I didn't come between you and your brother. You gave him away, so I took him. I don't have a little brother."

"Fine. Then take him. But I'm done taking orders from you! I'm not getting a job, and I'm not showing up for practice next week, either. *So get out.*"

Skip jotted down his name and phone number on a blank page of his pocket notebook. Tearing off the page, he handed it to his cousin. "Here, Trevor. Just in case you need me."

Trevor eyed him suspiciously. "I won't." But he slowly took the paper.

Skip pulled a twenty dollar bill from his trouser pocket and held out his hand to Trevor. In the darkness, Trevor couldn't see the money, but he likely would accept it if he grasped Skip's hand in friendship.

With his hands on his hips, Trevor glared at him. He didn't move.

Skip waited patiently. Just as he started to withdraw his hand, his cousin reached for it. Skip folded the money into his hand. Opening the door, he trotted up the basement steps and jumped into the car.

"What did he say?" asked Robby as they drove away.

"He accused me of coming between you two. At the restaurant, he said he'd do anything to get rid of you.

Well, now he's rid of you, and he's mad at me because you left him there alone."

Cassandra looked around. "Hey, Skip, where are we going? This isn't the way home."

"I thought we'd run by the hospital and see Johnny."

"Who's Johnny?" asked Robby.

"He's the cop who was chasing you guys the other day. He got broad-sided by a pick-up truck during the chase. Remember?" Skip glanced at Robby through his rear view mirror.

"Oh." Robby groaned and the color drained from his cheeks. "I felt awful when that happened. So did Damon. He started to pull over, but when Trevor started yelling like a maniac, we got scared and ran."

Skip pulled into the hospital parking lot and parked the car.

"Skip, may I wait in the car?" asked Robby.

"You don't want to meet Johnny?"

"What if he finds out that I was in the car that he was chasing?"

"You don't want him to know?"

"Would you?"

Skip laughed. "When you put it that way, no, I wouldn't."

The threesome hiked through the parking lot and into the hospital. Then they rode the elevator up to the fifth floor and strolled down the long corridor to Johnny's room. Since the door stood wide open, Skip entered without knocking.

"How do you feel?"

"I kind of hurt, but don't tell the nurse. She always wants to pump me full of pain medication."

"Hi, Johnny." Cassandra stepped around to the other side of his bed. "Boy, you look awful."

"I don't feel so good, either. But I'm glad you guys came by. I was getting kind of bored. Who's your friend?"

"This is Robby Thompson," said Skip. "I recruited him for our baseball team."

"It's nice to meet you, Robby." Johnny held out his unscathed right arm.

Robby gently shook his hand.

Johnny studied him for a moment, making Robby squirm in discomfort. Skip smiled as he watched them. He wasn't going to volunteer any information about Robby, but that didn't mean that Johnny wouldn't ask. Finally, Johnny turned to him.

"How did tryouts go? Those kids aren't giving you any trouble, are they?"

Skip looked away. *They were incorrigible. But how do I tell Johnny that I had trouble controlling them?*

"They behaved horribly," cried Cassandra.

Robby nodded. "They were rude and nasty and disrespectful."

"When's your next practice?"

"Next Saturday at ten thirty," said Skip.

"I'll be there. The hospital should release me within the next day or two."

"Johnny, when you get out of the hospital, you should be home recovering. Not at the ballpark. Jesse and I can handle those boys."

"Kid, that's my team. Of course, I trust you and Jesse, but unless I am providentially hindered, I shall be there next Saturday."

"Aye, aye, Coach."

"That's the point," said Johnny. "I never intended to coach those kids. I planned to turn them over to you anyway. Now, I ..." Johnny glanced at Cassandra and Robby and lowered his voice. "May I talk to you in private?"

Skip passed Cassandra the car keys. "Cassie, I need to see Johnny alone for a minute."

Cassandra took the hint. "Sure, Robby and I will wait for you in the car."

"I'll be there in a few minutes." When the two left the room, Skip closed the door and returned to Johnny's bedside.

"How was your honeymoon?"

Skip raised an eyebrow? "You had to ask me that in private?"

Johnny laughed. "No. I have another question, but since you're here, I thought I'd start with that one."

"Oh ... um ..." Skip winced, not knowing where to start.

"That bad, huh?"

"Yeah. Remember how those guys tried to keep me from marrying Cassandra? Well, you might say that the rest of the story played itself out on our honeymoon.

And it's a long story, but it has a happy ending. I'll tell you about it another time."

"Did you and Cassandra have any time alone?"

"No. My leave got canceled."

"I'm sorry to hear that. Now, about Robby, was he in the car I was chasing?"

"Yes. He's my cousin, but he doesn't know it, yet."

Chapter 21

A Warm Welcome

Cassandra glanced at her watch for the third time in two minutes. It was 3:25, and it was almost a thirty minute drive home from the hospital. Now she was concerned about getting Skip home late.

Let's face it, Lord. I have absolutely no control over this situation. So I'm going to do what I should have done from the start. I'm going to turn this situation over to you. Lord, would you get him home on time for this party. That would mean so much to his mom.

Sitting in the back seat of the car, Robby glanced toward the hospital's main entrance for the umpteenth time. What was taking Skip so long? He must be talking to Johnny about the trouble they had caused.

With a sigh, Robby wondered how he ever let Trevor talk him into leaving LA. His brother had gotten him into so much trouble here, it had him worried.

He was thankful to Skip for pulling him out of that dingy basement that they'd taken shelter in, but now he had no place to call his own. Not that the basement he'd lived in for the past three weeks even belonged to them. At some point, the real owner would reclaim it and then they'd be thrown out onto the street, if they weren't arrested. So he was extremely glad to be out of there. But what if they didn't welcome him at Skip's house? What would he do? Where would he go?

Robby glanced around the hospital parking lot and it hit him. He could call his mother collect from anywhere in the world, and she'd accept the charges. She would wire him enough money to get home, or she'd send him an airline ticket. Robby didn't have to stay here and feel unwanted or unloved. As soon as he got to a phone, he'd call home.

Robby jumped when the car door suddenly opened, and Skip slid behind the wheel. Cassandra had already inserted the car key into the ignition, so Skip simply started the car and backed out of his parking spot.

"What did Johnny want?" asked Cassandra.

"You're gonna laugh, but he asked about our honeymoon." Skip maneuvered through the parking lot and pulled out into traffic. "So, Robby, what's the real reason that you left home? Why did you follow Trevor out here?"

Robby sighed. "Ever since I can remember, Trevor's been my hero. I only came to Forest Valley to be with him. When dad passed away, Trevor suggested that we go see Uncle Stephen because he didn't have any kids, and we no longer had a father. I thought Trevor had received an invitation, so I came along with the understanding that Uncle Stephen was expecting us. But after we got here, I found out that Trevor didn't have an address for him. He befriended Damon the first day and has done nothing but cause trouble since he arrived. I was stuck because it took every nickel of my savings to get here. And then to find out from you that it was all a big fat lie."

"I'm sorry that you were coaxed into coming here under false pretense, Robby."

"Trevor told me a pack of lies, and I believed him. I trusted him! That burns me up. He didn't even want me to tell Mom where we were going, but I left her a note so she wouldn't worry."

"You love your mom a lot, don't you?"

"Yes, and she loves us so much. Skip, how could he do such a thing to her?"

"I don't know, Robby. If you had a chance to see your mom, what would you tell her?"

"That I love her. I know I broke her heart by running off. I wish I had a brother like you."

"How about cousin?" asked Skip.

Robby grinned. "Yeah, I'd even settle for cousin."

Skip turned into a driveway and cut the engine. Robby's heart started pounding. Now he wasn't so sure that this had been a wise decision. He slowly stepped from the car while Skip opened the door for Cassandra. They both looked peaceful and relaxed. So why was he uptight?

"Skip!" came the jubilant cry of little children.

Running down the sidewalk toward them were the four little girls Robby met when Cassandra had invited him swimming.

"Skip!"

Stepping around to the driver's door, Skip leaned against the car. The girls plowed into him.

"Where were you guys?" asked Skip.

"Melanie took us to the park," exclaimed Sandy.

Hoisting Scooter into his arms, and taking Cassandra's hand, he said, "Come on. Let's go in the house."

Cassandra said, "Smart move. They couldn't knock you down while you were standing next to the car."

"I know," said Skip. "That's why I stood here."

Those four little girls would have knocked him down? thought Robby. He watched as the girls trailed Skip into the house like he were the pied piper.

Breathing deeply, Robby collected all his courage and reluctantly followed them into the house.

Standing in the kitchen, Rose glanced around for any last minute details they may have forgotten. The beautifully-decorated birthday cake sat in the middle of the table, surrounded by paper plates, plastic ware, and napkins. The ice cream was in the freezer, barely three steps from where they stood. There were wrapped birthday gifts on the table for both her sweet young niece and nephew.

Erin glanced at the clock. "It's four o'clock exactly, and the pizza should be here any time."

"So should the kids," said Anita. "I told Melanie to have them home at four."

Just then, the ladies heard the front door open.

Anita peeked around the corner. "What timing. There are all eight of them."

"All eight?" echoed Erin. "But we should only have seven."

The ladies all stood in the kitchen doorway, but Rose's eyes widened at the sight of her son.

The moment Robby entered the house, he breathed in the most delicious smell. "Oo, I smell cake."

"So do I," said Skip. "Smells like chocolate."

A nice-looking lady greeted them as they filed into the house. "I see you brought home company," she said to Skip.

"Yeah, Mom. I want you to meet someone special. He needs a place to stay for a few weeks."

Skip's mother strolled over to him, her hand extended. "Well, you're certainly welcome here."

Robby relaxed. "Thank you, Ma'am. My name's Robby Thompson." He grasped her hand.

Her eyes widened in surprise. "Thompson?" She paused. "I'm Erin Shaughnessy."

Robby caught his breath and his face got hot. "Shaughnessy." He looked at Skip. "You called her 'mom!'"

Anger surged through Robby's veins. Trevor lied to him, and Skip deceived him. He trusted Skip. Withholding the truth was as bad as fabricating a lie. He felt betrayed again.

"Your name is Skip Shaughnessy. That's why you wouldn't tell us your last name. You knew that we were cousins. Didn't you?"

Skip grinned at him. "Robby, troublemakers always leave a trail. That trail led me to your names and the discovery of your relation to me. But I didn't think it wise to share that information with you at that time."

"Why not?" demanded Robby.

"Because I wasn't too sure you'd be cordial if you knew."

That statement stabbed Robby right through his heart. He wasn't being cordial. He was acting like his brother.

A soft, familiar voice interrupted his thoughts. "Robby?"

Recognizing his mom's voice, Robby glanced around and caught sight of his mother. *"Mom."*

The instant their eyes met, his mother flew across the room. "Robby." Rose pulled him into her arms and squeezed him tightly before releasing him.

"I told you I knew your mom," said Stephanie.

Robby gazed into his mother's watery brown eyes, filled with relief at the mere sight of him. "Mom, I'm so sorry for taking off on you like that. I've been miserable here."

"You look like you've lost weight," said Rose. "Have you had enough to eat? Where have you been staying? Where's your brother? I've been so worried about you both."

"Well, um ..." Robby glanced around at the rest of the family and decided they needed a little privacy. "Let's go for a walk, Mom, and I'll tell you all about it."

Just then, the doorbell rang.

"That's the pizza delivery driver," announced Erin.

Skip pulled open the door and saw the poor man almost buried under four large pizzas.

Robby started drooling. "Maybe we'll go for our walk after dinner."

Skip paid the driver and took the pizzas. "Robby, we just ate an hour ago. You can't possibly be hungry."

"I'm not. But do you know how long it's been since I've had pizza? I can make room for a piece or two."

"How about cake and ice cream?" asked Erin. "We're having a birthday party, and you're invited to stay."

"Yippee!" cried the girls, jumping up and down.

The Surprise Family Union

Hauling the pizzas into the dining room, where the table was already set, Skip breathed a sigh of relief. For a minute, he wasn't certain he'd made the right decision about bringing Robby home. Robby got downright hostile when he realized that they were cousins. Thank goodness for his Aunt Rose. She showed up at the right moment.

Chapter 22

In High Demand

Skip wasn't hungry, and all he wanted to do today was spend time alone with Cassandra. But one glance around the dining room told him that his mother and Aunt Rose had gone through an awful lot of work to put together a surprise birthday party for him and Stephie.

Colorful streamers everywhere. Pink and blue balloons. A beautifully decorated birthday cake with both his and Stephanie's name on it. Ice cream in the freezer. Presents.

Skip's eyes got big. *Presents?*

Cassandra looped her arm through his and cuddled up beside him. "Happy birthday," she whispered in his ear. Then she grabbed a piece of pizza.

Settling on a dining room chair, Skip surveyed the family activity. Cassandra and the girls interacted with

Robby, who seemed to feel right at home. The ladies enjoyed the party. After a round of the happy birthday chorus, everyone enjoyed cake and ice cream while Skip and Stephanie opened presents.

"Where's my present?" asked Scooter.

Skip pulled her into his lap. "You get presents on your birthday. In about a month, you'll turn four."

"Hey, Skip?"

Skip looked up at Robby.

"I owe you an apology. And I'm honored to call you my cousin. Thanks for reuniting me with my mom."

Rose joined her son. "I want to thank you, too, Skip. I really appreciate you." Turning to Robby, she said, "Let's go take that walk now. I want to know what's going on with Trevor."

As Rose and Robby headed out the front door, Erin strolled over to her son.

"Skip, you amazed me when you came home with Robby." Erin shook her head in disbelief. "I honestly didn't believe that was possible. You are just like your father."

Skip looked down to hide his embarrassment.

Stepping behind his chair, Cassandra wrapped her arms around him and whispered in his ear. "Can we continue my driving lessons?"

"Sure." *This is perfect. I can spend the rest of the afternoon with Cassandra. Just the two of us.* Skip stood and pulled her into his arms. "Mom, Cassandra and I are going for a drive, and we'll be back later."

"Okay."

Sandy pushed away her empty plate, chocolate icing all over her face, and scrambled over to her brother. "Can I come?"

"No, sweetheart, not this time. Cassandra is driving, and you will be much safer in the house."

"Skip!"

"Well, it's true. Isn't it?"

Cassandra giggled. "Yes, but you didn't have to say it."

Skip kissed her, and her frustration melted right before his eyes. "Sorry." Grasping her hand, he led her out the front door.

"See ya all later," he called with a wave.

Skip's twelve-hour workdays resumed on Sunday morning. With Robby at his house, Trevor was alone, so Skip cruised through the area a time or two to see what he was up to. He also checked on Damon. He discovered that Damon was at work, but he couldn't locate Trevor. He stopped by his pad a couple of times, but his cousin wasn't there.

Skip hoped he was staying out of trouble. He hadn't received any radio calls regarding mischievous activity or petty theft, so that was good. In fact, even for a Sunday, the town seemed unusually quiet.

After cruising around for a couple of hours, his radio dead silent, Skip finally pulled into the hospital parking lot and radioed dispatch of his location. Strolling through the lobby, he caught the elevator up to Johnny's floor.

With four active little sisters demanding his attention, his aunt and cousin desiring to develop a relationship with him, and his young bride requiring he give her quality time, Skip found his time in constant demand and his home life a continuous bustle of activity. The only one who didn't seem to require his attention was his mother. She worked hard to divert his little sisters' attention from him, and sometimes she succeeded. Between his job and family, Skip ran practically non-stop.

Most of his duty days were equally as busy since he responded to one radio call after another. Work was so hectic, he didn't have the opportunity to follow up with either Damon or Trevor, but he didn't cross paths with them in the performance of his duty. He wondered where they were and what they were up to, but he was too tired to try to locate them after work, so he let it go. Hopefully, he would see them at practice on Saturday, and he could talk to them at that time.

By Wednesday, a few officers had recovered from the flu enough to return to work, so those who had endured the longest shifts for the greatest duration finally found relief when their hours were reduced. Unfortunately for Skip, he wasn't among them. He pulled another twelve-hour shift on Wednesday, and after work he headed straight to church for the midweek service.

Still in uniform, Skip slid in beside Cassandra. He was late again. Cassandra silently slipped her hand into his and snuggled up to him as the pastor stepped up to the pulpit and opened his Bible.

As tired as he was, Skip hated to miss church. He feared that he'd miss a vital message that God had for him. And tonight's message seemed to be aimed at his heart. God spoke to him about loving his family and his two long lost cousins, so he was glad he'd gone.

When Skip finally got home, it was only 8:30, but he could hardly keep his eyes open, so he marched upstairs to bed. Cassandra trailed him into the bedroom.

"Aw, Skip, you're not going to bed all ready. I haven't seen you all day."

Skip yawned, barely able to keep his eyes open as he kicked off his shoes and changed into his pajamas. "I'm sorry, Cassandra, but I'm so tired, and I need good rest to be effective on the street."

Cassandra heaved an exaggerated sigh. "How much longer will you be on this shift?"

"Not much longer. The flu epidemic has just about run its course, and everyone afflicted will soon be back at work. But a couple of the guys came back today, so they're starting to cut hours. Jesse's back on eight hours."

"But not you? That's not fair."

"I know you hate this shift I'm on. I'm not crazy about it myself, but while we were visiting your aunt and uncle, Jesse was pulling sixteen-hour days. Do you really think it's fair to reduce my hours first?"

Tears welled up in her eyes and she buried her face in his pajama shirt. "I'm sorry. I just miss you so much. No, of course, it wouldn't be fair."

"Hopefully, I'll be back with Jesse by the end of the week." Skip cuddled her, running his fingers through her long, auburn hair.

"Did you eat before going to church?" asked Cassandra. "Your stomach is growling."

"Eat?" Skip raised an eyebrow. "No wonder I'm so hungry. I missed dinner."

"You want something light before you go to bed? Say, a banana and a glass of milk?"

Skip could go to bed on an empty stomach, and it wouldn't keep him awake, but if he ate a little something, he could spend a few minutes with Cassandra, and that would make her happy.

"That sounds great, Cassandra. Thank you."

Skip glanced at the clock as he followed her from the bedroom. Eight forty-five. By the time he climbed into bed, it was nine thirty. Cassandra crawled in beside him, and he pulled her into his arms.

The next thing he knew, his mother was shaking him. His initial concern was work. He must have overslept, but one glance at the clock told him differently. It was only midnight.

"What's wrong, Mom?"

"Skip, I'm sorry to wake you, but Trevor's on the phone. He wants to talk to you."

Trevor's calling at this hour? That can't be good.

Chapter 23

The Midnight Phone Call

Skip scooted out from under Cassandra and slid off the bed. "Thanks, Mom. I'll grab it down in the kitchen so you can go back to bed."

Still half asleep, he rubbed his eyes and rolled out of bed. Skip trotted down the stairs, grabbing the receiver to the wall-mounted phone.

"Hello?" He spoke barely above a whisper.

"Skip, is that you?"

"Mm-hmm. Trevor, do you know how late it is?"

Trevor sighed. "Yes. I'm sorry for waking you up, but I didn't know who else to call. I got arrested tonight. Would you come bail me out?"

"I don't think so. If I bail you out, I am accepting responsibility for you, and you've already made it very clear that you have no intentions of listening to me or doing anything I tell you to." Skip yawned. "Goodnight. I'm going back to bed." Skip started to hang up, but Trevor's frightened plea stopped him.

"No, Skip, please don't hang up. I'm sorry for what I said. I didn't mean it. I'll do everything you tell me to. But I don't want to spend the night in jail. It would absolutely crush my mother if she found out."

Skip grimaced at the mention of his Aunt Rose. In the short time he'd known her, he had grown very fond of her and would do just about anything to protect her. And strange as it seemed, Trevor had no way of knowing that Skip knew his mother, or that his concern for her might be the only thing to touch his heart in the middle of the night.

"Why are you just now thinking of how your actions will affect your mother? Shouldn't you have given that some thought before you landed in jail?"

"I should have. You warned me." Trevor sighed and his voice cracked. "All I can say is, I'm sorry." Trevor hung up.

Now wide awake, Skip slowly hung up the phone and turned to see his mother standing in the doorway.

"He got arrested?" gasped Erin.

Sinking wearily onto a kitchen chair, Skip dropped his head into his hands. "And he wants me to bail him out."

"It might do him good to sit in jail for a day or two."

"I was thinking the same thing, but how do you suppose Aunt Rose will take it when she finds out?"

With a groan, Erin sat down beside Skip. "Oh, Skip, it will kill her, just like it would do to me if you got arrested for breaking the law."

Skip rose to his feet and kissed his mother's cheek. "I love you, Mom. Why don't you go back to bed. I'll take care of Trevor." Trotting up the stairs, he changed out of his pajamas, grabbed his glasses, and headed out the door.

Unable to quit yawning, Skip tried to rub the fatigue from his eyes before entering the police station.

"Skip, what are you doing here at this hour?" asked Sergeant Kevin McAllister.

"I came to bail Trevor Thompson out of jail." Skip stifled a yawn. "What was he arrested for?"

"Stealing apples."

"May I see the complaint?"

Kevin handed Skip the report, and he reviewed it.

"That's what I thought – same lady who complained last week. I wonder if she'd drop the charges if he paid for the apples." Skip grabbed the phone and punched in her number.

"Skip, are you crazy? It's one o'clock in the morning."

"Hello?" An irritated female voice shot over the line.

"Ma'am, this is Officer Skip Shaughnessy with the Forest Valley Police Department. I took your theft report last week."

Her voice softened. "I remember. What can I do for you, Officer Shaughnessy?"

"I'm calling about the boy who was arrested tonight for stealing your apples. Would you be willing to drop the charges if he paid for them?"

There was a pause on the other end of the line. "Yes, providing I have the money tonight and his assurance that he'll stay off my property from now on."

"You'll have it. He'll be by in a little bit to make restitution."

Trevor lay on the hard bunk in the dimly-lit cell staring up at the ceiling. Boy, had he made a mess of things. He abandoned his mother at a time she needed him. He drove away his brother by his attitude and harsh words. Damon was staying out of trouble since Skip showed up at his house unexpectedly and blackmailed him into playing baseball. He had no one to turn to except Skip, but Skip refused to bail him out.

I don't think so, Trevor. If I bail you out, I am accepting responsibility for you, and you've already made it very clear that you have no intentions of listening to me or doing anything I tell you to.

Trevor blinked back a tear. What Skip said was true.

I have nothing to say to you. You're not my boss, and you have no right to tell me where I can go and what I can do. Now, you've come between me and my brother. Well, I'm done taking orders from you. I'm not getting a job, and I'm not showing up for practice next week, either. So get out.

No wonder Skip wouldn't bail him out. He could place a collect call to his mother in Los Angeles. She'd accept the charges from him, but how could he tell her that he'd been arrested? Skip was right about that, too.

Why are you just now thinking of how your actions will affect your mother? Shouldn't you have given that some thought before you landed in jail?

Trevor sighed. "Lord, what happened? How did I get to this point in my life?"

Troublemakers always leave a trail. Yours led to jail.

Rattling keys grabbed his attention, and he sat up on the bunk just as his cell door opened.

"Your bond has been posted." The third shift police officer ushered him out.

"Who posted it?" asked Trevor.

"Don't you know? You only made one phone call."

Skip. Trevor trailed the officer to the front office where Skip was signing papers.

Laying down the pen, Skip made brief eye contact with him and motioned him out of the office. "Thanks, fellows. See you in a few hours."

Hands in his pockets, Trevor stared down at the floor as he trailed Skip out of the police station to the car. Fully expecting a lecture, Trevor wearily dropped into the front passenger's seat and buckled in. But when Skip didn't say anything, he leaned back and closed his eyes for the duration of the ride. He didn't open them again until he felt the car turn into a driveway.

A driveway? He didn't have a driveway.

Trevor glanced around. They were parked in front of someone's house. Maybe Skip lived here and Trevor would get to sleep on a soft bed tonight. "Where are we?"

"The house where you stole the apples."

"Oh. I always went over the back fence, so I didn't know what the front of the house looked like, but why did we come here?"

"Because if you pay that lady for the apples you took, she'll drop the charges against you."

"What if I refuse?" demanded Trevor.

"Then you will no longer be my problem, because I'll take you back to jail."

Trevor swallowed hard and glanced away. "Skip, I ... I don't have any money."

"What happened to the twenty I gave you?"

"I spent it. A guy has to eat, ya know. That's why I stole her apples. I ran out of money."

"I have some money. Go find out how much you owe her."

"Do I have to?"

"Not if you'd prefer jail."

"Would you come with me?" asked Trevor.

"Nope. This is something you have to do on your own."

Trevor slowly stepped from the car. Swallowing hard, he glanced back at Skip, who had crossed his arms over the steering wheel and rested his head on them.

Collecting his courage, Trevor dragged himself up the walkway and knocked on the door.

The door jerked open, and a middle-aged woman wearing a bathrobe stepped outside to talk to him. "Well, it took you long enough to get here."

"Sorry. Um, h-h-how much do I owe you for the apples?" asked Trevor.

"I think twenty dollars ought to cover it."

"T-t-twenty dollars! But I only took four apples."

"This last time you only took four apples. This is the fourth time you've raided my tree, and I'm guessing that all together you've robbed me of at least twenty dollars worth of apples, if not more. Now, if you expect me to drop the charges, then you'll fork over twenty dollars."

Trevor swallowed hard and glanced back at the car. How could he ask Skip for that much money?

Hustling back to the car, Trevor yanked open the front passenger's door and startled Skip. Skip bolted upright as Trevor leaned into the car. "She wants twenty dollars."

Skip withdrew his wallet and handed Trevor a twenty-dollar bill. Trevor didn't know what to think of that. After all the trouble he'd caused, Skip was handing him another twenty dollar bill. Slowly taking the money, Trevor returned to the lady waiting at the door and handed her the money.

"Young man, I hope you appreciate the boy who bailed you out of jail in the middle of the night and forked over the money to cover the cost of your theft.

He's been a real friend to you. What kind have you been to him?"

I haven't been a friend to him. I haven't tried to be a friend to him.

Pivoting, Trevor marched back to the car and jumped in beside Skip. Skip rubbed his eyes and started the car, carefully backing out of the driveway. Trevor sat quietly. He glanced at Skip, expecting to get chewed out for his actions, but Skip didn't say a word.

Finally, Skip broke the silence. "How's your job hunt coming?" He turned into the alley and stopped the car right at Trevor's door. Shifting to park, he let the car idle.

"Well, it's not really. I ... um ..."

"Haven't looked too hard, huh?"

"No."

"Well, hang in there. Keep looking. If I can help, give me a call."

Trevor forced a smile. "Thanks."

"Do you need a ride to practice on Saturday?"

"I could use one."

"I'll be here around ten o'clock," said Skip. "See you then."

Trevor jumped from the car, and Skip drove off. Frozen to his spot, he watched Skip's car cruise down the long alley and round the corner. He had no desire to spend another night in that dark and dingy basement. At least not by himself. If Robby were here, it might be tolerable, because then it wouldn't be so quiet. He never thought he'd feel this way, but he missed his brother's company, and he was starting to feel homesick. He was ready to go back to LA, and he wondered if his mother would welcome him home.

Chapter 24

Robby's Hero

By the time Skip reached home, it was almost three o'clock. His mother yawned and sat up on the sofa when he came in. Although Skip encouraged her to go to bed and get some sleep, she always waited up for him.

"I'm home, Mom." Skip bolted the front door. "Goodnight." He trotted up to his room and changed into his pajamas before crawling into bed beside Cassandra.

Skip jumped when his alarm sounded. Turning it off, he dragged himself out of bed and started getting ready for work. As tired as he was from the three hour interruption to his sleep, he thanked the Lord for the four and a half hours that he did get.

Sitting on the bed to tie his boots, Skip talked to the Lord. "Jesus, send an angel to guard and protect me today. Give me strength and wisdom to make godly decisions in everything I do, and provide me with the energy to get through the day."

Skip kissed Cassandra and stroked her soft cheek. She smiled in her sleep but didn't open her eyes. Slipping out of the room, he shut the door behind him and tiptoed down the stairs, trying not to rouse the entire household by thumping down the hardwood steps with his boots. With only a few minutes to spare, Skip spent that time in prayer before grabbing a banana for breakfast and heading out the door.

Stephanie's tenth birthday was four days ago, and Skip had been so busy that he'd forgotten to get her a birthday present. Not that she'd noticed. Between Robby's unexpected visit and the pile of gifts that Aunt Rose and Mom had bought for her, she didn't think to ask him which present was from him. But he'd forgotten to buy her something this year. And that bothered him.

The first opportunity he had, Skip went code six at the art supply store and bought his sister an expensive drawing set. Stephanie was a little artist, and she didn't seem to have the right kind of pencils to do her sketches.

Skip asked the store to gift wrap it for him. When he finally got home a little past seven, the only one waiting for him was Cassandra.

She rushed into his arms and planted her lips against his the moment he strolled through the door.

"Oh, I missed you. I'm glad you're home. Is that gift for me?"

"No, it's for Stephanie. This is a late birthday present. Where is Stephanie?" Skip bolted the front door and glanced around the quiet house. "In fact, where is everybody?"

"The girls are out in the backyard playing ball with Robby. Your mom and Aunt Rose are also out back. They're just sitting in a couple of lawn chairs talking while they watch the kids play ball."

Cassandra kissed him again. "I'll bet you're starved. Come in the kitchen and I'll warm your supper."

Skip followed Cassandra into the kitchen and sat down at the table. He wasn't used to the solitude. Ordinarily, his attention was in high demand, especially from his young sisters. But with Aunt Rose and Robby here, he might even get to enjoy Cassandra's company without constant interruptions.

After filling his tummy, Skip left Stephanie's gift-wrapped package on the table and headed up the stairs with Cassandra.

"You gotta be tired," said Cassandra. "Your mom told me about the three hour interruption to your sleep last night."

Skip yawned. "Well, if you don't object, I'm going to bed now."

Just then, Stephanie screamed. "Skip!" She bounded up the stairs and into his arms. "Thank you. That was the best present ever."

Skip worked twelve-hour days all week, but by Saturday most of the officers had returned to work, so Captain Kramer gave him the entire weekend off, with an end to his long duty days. That was the best birthday present he received.

Trevor found the isolation of his dark and silent basement dwelling increasingly undesirable. He saw Damon far less often than he wanted, and he hadn't seen Robby in a week. Sleeping on the concrete floor was becoming more difficult each night and he was waking up with tremendous backaches and headaches. Doing what he wanted when he wanted had lost its appeal, and he was starting to live for things he'd always taken for granted before – a hot shower and a comfortable bed, a good meal and good company, family and friends. So when Saturday finally arrived, Trevor looked forward to seeing his brother, visiting with Damon, and helping Skip with the equipment.

Tearing the wrapper from a gigantic, individually wrapped muffin and grabbing a bottle of water, Trevor trotted up the steps into the alley to wait for Skip. He stepped outside a little early, and the bright sunshine warmed his disposition. He had finished his muffin and downed half his bottle of water when Skip pulled up.

Trevor jumped into the back seat beside Robby. "Good morning," he said to Skip and Cassandra. Then he turned to his brother. "Hi, Robby."

Robby stared out the opposite window. "Hi, Trev."

Trevor's heart sank. He had looked forward all week to seeing Robby, and his brother wasn't happy to see him at all. With pursed lips, Trevor glanced hurtfully at Skip. *He must have blabbed to Robby about bailing me out of jail.*

When they arrived at the park, Trevor saw some guy in a wheelchair there talking to Skip's friend, Jesse, and a few of the other boys. Skip parked the car, they gathered up the equipment, and they headed over to join the others.

"Hi, Johnny, you're looking good," said Skip. "How do you feel?"

"I've had better days," said Johnny. "Who's your friend?"

"Oh, this is Trevor Thompson. And you've already met his brother, Robby." Skip turned to Trevor. "I'd like you to meet, Johnny. He's more than my friend. He's kind of like my dad."

Trevor shook his hand. "Pleased to meet you."

Although Johnny was in a wheelchair, Trevor could tell that he was glad to be there. And as the rest of the boys arrived, they all gathered around to see how he was doing, so Trevor knew that they were already acquainted with him.

Johnny took roll call before turning them over to Skip. With Johnny's presence, Trevor noticed that the boys showed Skip respect for his leadership position. He got them working on batting skills, stealing bases, and sliding.

While Skip worked with the team, Trevor tried to talk to Robby, but his brother avoided him. Every time he got within a few feet, Robby turned and walked away from him. The third time it happened, Trevor knew it wasn't coincidental.

"Robby, what's the matter with you?" He hastily closed the gap and confronted Robby face to face. "Since you've moved in with ... with ... with that meddling cop you won't even talk to me."

"Don't you talk about Skip like that!" growled Robby through clenched teeth. "He's my friend. And he's been more of a friend to me in a week than you've been in an entire lifetime."

"He's not a friend. He's a traitor. Because a friend knows when to keep his mouth shut."

Robby cocked his head. "Keep his mouth shut? About what? What are you talking about?"

"You know perfectly well what I'm talking about."

With a confused look, Robby shook his head. "Honestly, I don't."

"Skip didn't tell you what happened on Wednesday night?"

Robby shook his head. "No. What happened? Tell me."

"He bailed me out of some trouble. The way you were acting, I thought he told you."

"Skip never said a word about it. I was avoiding you because of the things you said last week. You're my hero, Trevor. I would do anything to make you proud of me, and I was deeply hurt by your rejection. You were only using me to hurt Mom."

Trevor raised an eyebrow. *I'm Robby's hero? All this time he's been trying to please me?* "Oh, Robby, I'm so sorry. Can you ever forgive me? I didn't mean those things I said last week. I was just hurt that Mom told me to get a job, but not you. I don't need to work. She has enough money to support us all."

"I already had a job lined up. I was supposed to start last Monday."

"You were? Did Mom make you get it?"

Robby laughed. "No, I want to work. I want to be independent. To do something great with my life like Mom did."

Trevor never looked at it that way before. "Hey, it's kind of lonely in that dark old basement by myself. I miss your company. How about coming back."

"No way. At Skip's house there's a lot more light, a place to shower and clean up, and I get regular meals. Plus, sleeping on the sofa is a lot more comfortable than that old concrete. Why don't you come stay with us?"

"I can't do that. I haven't been invited."

"So I'm inviting you."

"You can't invite me. It's not your house."

"Skip really wouldn't mind, Trevor. And his mom would welcome you just like she welcomed me."

"No, thanks. I don't want to be a burden on anyone."

"How are you eating?" asked Robby. "Have you gotten a job yet?"

"Well, not exactly. But after what happened Wednesday, I decided I'd better do something, so I've picked up some odd jobs here and there for a few bucks. It's not much, but it does buy me a little grub."

"Hey, Robby, are you practicing with us?" called Skip.

"I'm coming." Pulling a crumpled one-dollar bill and a pen from his pocket, Robby smoothed out the bill and jotted down Skip's address on the border of it. "Here. This is all I had to write on." He thrust the bill into Trevor's hand. "In case you change your mind." Spinning around, Robby grabbed his mitt and darted onto the field.

Skip and Jesse worked the boys for almost three hours before finally releasing them for the day.

As they gathered around the water cooler guzzling down cup after cup of cold water, Johnny called out, "Okay, fellows, I have some important things to talk to you about, so have a seat on the bleachers and give me your attention for about five minutes."

The boys piled onto the bleachers and looked at Johnny.

"I've arranged for you to play Alcova three weeks from today. That will give you a reason to train hard and prepare. Also, I've been rounding up sponsors for your team, and I have just about enough money in donations to purchase uniforms."

"Uniforms." The boys all started talking at once.

"We'll look like a real team."

"Yeah."

Johnny held up his hands to settle them down. "This game will be announced all over town, and a lot of people will come to cheer you on. Skip, when is their next practice?"

"Monday at five o'clock."

"We'll be here." The boys scattered, chattering excitedly as they headed off in different directions.

Skip couldn't believe the sudden change in their demeanors. And that would reflect in their efforts on Monday. He was already looking forward to their next practice.

Chapter 25

Help Wanted

Since Robby had come back into her life, Rose was more at peace. Still, she found it increasingly difficult to keep her mind off her wayward son – wondering if Trevor was making good decisions. Did he have enough to eat? Was he staying out of trouble? She wanted Skip to invite him to church, but she didn't think he'd welcome her presence. Nor would he respond well when he learned that Skip was part of his family.

On Sunday afternoon, while the three little ones were napping, the others pulled out the monopoly game. But Erin and Rose sat down to chat over coffee.

"Erin, I'm so thankful for Skip bringing Robby back to me. I hope he can reach Trevor."

"He's trying, Rose, but things like that take time."

Rose sipped her coffee. "I know they do, and I appreciate all he's done. But somehow, I don't feel it's enough. Could we pray again?"

"Certainly. Stephen was instrumental in steering many kids away from trouble. And he did a lot of it on his knees."

"That sounds like Stephen. He always had a heart for others."

"Yes, he did," said Erin. "And Skip is just like his father."

Holding hands, the ladies bowed their heads and prayed earnestly for Trevor Thompson. Tears trickled down her cheeks as Erin asked the Lord to bless Skip with God's guidance and wisdom in dealing with him.

"Skip's the only one who's been able to connect with him in any way. Strengthen him and fill him with Your Holy Spirit and power that he might guide Trevor back to You and his family..."

After enjoying a long, hot shower, Trevor dressed in Damon's clothes while all of his were taking a bath of their own in the washing machine. He ran a comb through his unkempt hair and left the steamy bathroom to join his friend downstairs in the kitchen, whipping up some pancakes.

Still barefoot, Trevor pulled up a bar stool and sat down at the tall kitchen counter.

"You hungry?" Damon set a plate of golden-brown pancakes on the counter beside the syrup and butter.

Settling on the bar stool on the opposite side of the counter, he and Trevor served themselves and started to eat.

"I thought your mom didn't like me. I still can't believe that she let me come over to shower and do laundry. And boy, did I need a shower. I could smell myself."

"I told her that you're one of my teammates."

"So what difference does that make?" asked Trevor.

"Since I joined the team, I've been staying out of trouble. So she figures that I'm developing some good associations there, and that you're one of them."

Trevor laughed. "Yeah, if she only knew the truth."

"The truth is, I asked Skip to put me on the team because I wanted to play."

"You did what? Damon, you're only there at all because he blackmailed you."

Damon shrugged. "Hey, I've had fun playing baseball. Skip's a great coach. I've rearranged my work schedule to make all the practices. It's giving me something to look forward to, and it's keeping me out of trouble. It's the best thing that's happened to me in a long time. I'm sorry that you don't like it, but my mom sees a change in me as a result, and that is why she allowed you to come shower and do laundry."

Trevor sighed. "You've changed. Robby's changed."

"Change isn't a bad thing, ya know. Whether or not you realize it, you've changed, too. Hey, have you and Robby separated? I don't see you together anymore."

"Yeah, he's been staying with Skip, and he invited me to come stay there, too. But something's not right with that invitation. How can he invite me to someone else's home with such confidence? He seemed certain that I would be welcomed."

"That is strange," said Damon. "Did you ever find out Skip's last name?"

Trevor grinned. "No, but his name might answer some of my questions, and I think I know how to get it."

On Monday morning, Trevor hiked to the police station. Pulling open the door, he crossed the lobby to the large sheet of bullet-proof glass.

"May I help you?" asked the female clerk on the other side of the glass.

"I need to see Officer Skip ... um ..." Trevor snapped his fingers like he was trying to remember the last name.

"Shaughnessy."

Trevor gasped at the mention of that name. *Shaughnessy. Why, that rat fink is the son of my Uncle Stephen.*

"He's out on patrol right now. Would you like for me to radio him to meet you at the station?"

"No, that's all right." Trevor pushed through the door and left the police station. *Boy, that steams me up. He deceived me. Wait until I get my hands on him.*

Thrusting his hands deep into his pockets, Trevor wandered through downtown, wondering how to get back at Skip. A 'Help Wanted' sign caught his attention. He stopped to admire the handsome, new motorcycles that lined the front of the store.

So they're looking for help. Well, they're not getting any from me. I refuse to get a job and give Skip the satisfaction.

Kicking a small stone into the street, he stomped away. A sudden thought hit him, and he looked back at the motorcycle shop. Trevor grinned. Doing an about face, he entered the store.

On second thought, maybe a job in a motorcycle store is just what I need.

Trevor wandered through the showroom floor, dreaming of the day one of those motorcycles would be his. He'd wanted a motorcycle since his tenth birthday. His dad used to take him for rides on his motorcycle, and he even taught Trevor how to handle and maneuver the bike when he was fifteen. His dad had told him that he'd buy Trevor a motorcycle on his eighteenth birthday. But his dad died before his eighteenth birthday. And that promise had become nothing more than a dream that blew away in the wind.

A tall, muscular man approached him. "May I help you? Are you looking for any particular brand or model?"

Trevor smiled at him. He wanted a job in this store, so he had to pull out all the charm. And he knew just how to do it. He'd been watching Skip.

"No, sir. I would love to own a motorcycle, but I just don't have any way to pay for it. I actually came in because I saw your 'help wanted' sign."

"Hmm, you're looking for a job, huh? Well, I certainly could use the help. But I was actually looking for someone a little older. Do you have any experience working in a motorcycle shop?"

"No, sir, but I'm a real fast learner. My name is Trevor Thompson. And I'm very responsible. If you'll give me a chance, you'll see what a great asset I could be. May I fill out a job application?"

"Yeah, I suppose it couldn't hurt. Wait here."

A moment later, the man returned with a job application in his hand.

"Thank you, sir." Trevor took the application and left the shop. Crossing the street, he entered the coffee shop. He didn't have a lot of money on him, but he had enough for a cup of coffee and a doughnut. After ordering, he sat down at a small, round table with his snack, pulled out his pen, and looked at the application.

He'd been so adamant about living off his mother's wealth that he'd never even looked at a job application before.

Oh, my, thought Trevor. *I hope I can figure this thing out.*

He didn't have an address, so he put down Damon's. He'd never held a job before, so he wrote down a fictitious business and gave it a California address. That way, his new boss couldn't contact them. He didn't know his social security number, but his card was in his wallet, so that part was easy. The application asked what kind of salary he was looking for.

Trevor thought, *I get to pick my own salary? Wow!* So he wrote down $100 / hour.

Then it asked for references.

Trevor crinkled his nose. "References? What are references?"

Glancing around the small coffee house, Trevor spotted a young woman sitting at another table reading a book, so he approached her. "Excuse me, Ma'am. I'm trying to fill out a job application and they asked for references. What are references?"

The lady started laughing. "That means they want to know if you can give them the names of some people who know you."

"Oh. Thanks." Trevor jotted down Damon's name. With a grin, he thought about Skip. "Why not?" So he wrote down Skip's name.

He finally signed his application. Trevor popped the last bit of doughnut into his mouth, finished his coffee, and tossed his trash into the can. Then he picked up his completed application and returned to the motorcycle shop to turn it in.

"Wow, that was fast," said the shop owner. He glanced over Trevor's application and raised an eyebrow. "You put down Skip for a reference? Well, if Skip knows you, that's good enough for me. My only concern is your asking pay. Why did you put down $100 an hour?"

"Well, you asked how much I wanted?"

The man laughed. "That's true. But I can't afford $100 an hour. How about if we compromise, and I'll pay you $6.00 an hour, with a commission on every motorcycle you sell. By the way, my name is Adam Cryder."

Trevor shook his hand. "Can I start today?"

"Well, we have some paperwork to complete and tax forms to fill out before it's official. So let's try to take care of all that today, and you can start tomorrow."

"Thank you, sir," said Trevor. His plan to get back at Skip was beginning to take shape.

Skip had only three weeks to get his team ready for the game against Alcova. The big game was scheduled for Saturday, July twenty-second at noon. Since he and Jesse were back on regular shift, they scheduled practice for four times a week – Monday, Tuesday, Friday, and Saturday.

Johnny came to every practice to cheer on the boys and lend support.

Although Trevor attended every practice, Skip detected a change in his demeanor. Whereas before his cousin was beginning to open up to him, now he appeared cold and unsociable, even angry. Skip tried to address it, but Trevor refused to talk to him.

Robby joined his brother in the dugout. "What's up, Trev? You look really irritable today."

Trevor glared at him. "As if you don't know."

"Know what? I have no idea what you're talking about."

"Yeah, yeah." Trevor leaped to his feet. *"You* know. And I'm not stupid. I know you know." Trevor left the dugout and shoved Skip aside as he was on his way in.

Skip chased after him. "Hey, Trevor, what's with you? I thought we were friends."

"Well, you thought wrong!" yelled Trevor. "So just leave me alone! I'll be back to help you pack up the equipment."

With his hands on his hips, Skip shook his head and watched Trevor storm off. Leaving his concern for Trevor, he returned to the infield. His team needed some fielding practice, so Skip snatched up the bat and ball. Tossing the ball into the air, he smacked it into the field.

For the next hour, he belted the ball in different directions, hitting grounders and pop flies all over the field. The boys fielded the ball and fired it to first.

They finished up with some batting practice.

Robby and Damon helped Skip gather up the equipment and load it into the back of his car.

"Where's Trevor?" asked Damon. "Isn't this his job?"

"It is," said Skip. "I hate to say it, but Trevor is headed for big trouble if he keeps going in this direction."

Chapter 26

Trevor's Devious Plan

Trevor loved motorcycles and found his job a pure delight. Mr. Cryder taught him all about the different brands and models of each type of bike. He showed Trevor the manual that contained the comprehensive data on each motorcycle, how to look up the retail price, their lowest sale price, and their original purchase price. Besides the showroom floor with almost two dozen brand new motorcycles, they also had a store that sold plenty of motorcycle accessories.

True to his word, Trevor impressed Mr. Cryder with how eager he was to learn and how quickly he learned. The first day, two different customers came in at two different times. Trevor tagged along as Mr. Cryder greeted each of them, helped each man find the type of motorcycle he was looking for and answered all his questions.

After the prospective customer had left the store, Trevor turned to his boss. "You didn't sell that guy a bike."

"He wasn't ready to buy today. But I have a feeling he'll be back. Come on, let's go do some stocking. I'll show you where everything is."

Although Mr. Cryder's motorcycle store closed at six o'clock, he released Trevor at five. So Trevor grabbed a bite to eat and headed to the ballpark.

With each practice, Skip witnessed a steady transformation of his team as the boys not only showed him more respect, but their playing improved. Every practice, Skip worked on a specific area with them. He taught the boys some crucial signals.

"After you hit the ball, watch me. You don't have time to look around to see where the ball is. Just look at me. If I think you have time to get to the next base, I'll signal you to keep running."

"Aye, coach."

Skip caught Trevor's late arrival out of the corner of his eye. "Now let's do some batting practice."

"Yay!" The boys cheered. It was their favorite part of the game, and Skip knew that they didn't get to bat half as much as they wanted to.

"All right, fellows. Here's what we're doing. Jesse has put together the batting order, and that's the order in which you're batting today. We'll adjust it as needed. Everyone else will be in the field. As batter, your job is get a base hit. Now for those in the field – your job is to get him out. Keep him from making it to first."

"What? We're to throw out our own team member?" cried Jeff, the team's first baseman.

"For the purpose of this practice, the batter is not part of your team. In the field, you guys work as a team. When you're at bat, remember, your team is in the dugout. Now this is batting practice, so whether or not you make it to base safely, when the next batter comes to bat, you head to the field. And remember to watch me for signals because the batter's turn is not over until he's out or safely on base." Skip looked over at Robby. "And your job as pitcher is to strike him out if you can. Remember, for this practice, the batter represents a player from the other team. Now, Jesse's going to read off the batting order, So pay attention."

"Aye, aye, coach."

For two hours, the boys worked out. When it was Robby's turn at bat, Skip pitched for him. Skip only knew one pitch – the fast ball – but that's all he needed to strike out Robby.

"Hey, that's not fair," complained Robby as he returned to the pitcher's mound. "You almost signed with a major league team. I'll never get a hit with you pitching to me. You throw too fast."

"Sure, you will," said Skip. "And once you start hitting my pitches, you'll be able to hit anything the Alcova pitcher throws at you."

Jesse covered for the catcher when it was his turn at bat.

Each of the boys were able to bat three times in that two hour time slot. By the end of practice, their fielding had improved tremendously, and so had Robby's pitching.

"Hm." Skip rubbed his chin. "I think our next practice will be held at the batting cages."

As practice concluded, the boys all gathered around Skip.

"Hey, were you really offered a contract to play in the majors?" asked Victor, the shortstop.

"Yeah, I was a junior in high school."

"And you turned it down?"

"Unfortunately, the timing wasn't right." Skip glanced around for Trevor to see if he was helping with the equipment, but he'd already left the ballpark.

By Trevor's second week on the job, he was comfortable running Mr. Cryder's store and ringing out customers. He'd also learned how to warmly welcome potential motorcycle buyers into the showroom and get them interested in a particular motorcycle. But Trevor didn't know how to make the sale himself yet, so he had to interrupt Mr. Cryder, who was in his office doing paperwork.

Mr. Cryder never minded an interruption that resulted in a motorcycle sale. He took the opportunity to walk Trevor through the process, and they split the commission.

When things got slow, Trevor strolled through the showroom, dusting off the shiny new motorcycles. He paused outside Mr. Cryder's office door when he heard his boss on the phone.

"I don't blame you, Aaron. Nor do I hold it against you. I mean, let's face it. Karen is the baby of the family, the last to get married, and the only girl in a houseful of boys. And nobody wants to miss her wedding." Adam sighed. "And your mother and I are looking forward to this more than anybody. I'll just have to close my business on that day ... Yeah, I did hire help, but he's so young, still learning, and I don't know if I trust him enough to leave him here alone ... That's true. Her wedding is still about ten days away. That'll give Trevor another week to get totally comfortable in this job. Then I can decide at that time. Talk to you later."

Mr. Cryder hung up the phone and Trevor stepped into his office. "So when's Karen's wedding?" he asked.

"Were you eavesdropping?"

"Well, I wasn't trying to. It's kinda quiet out here, so I was just dusting the motorcycles. Is Karen your daughter?"

"Yes, and her wedding is July twenty-first at 5:00."

The night before the big game against Alcova. What an incredible opportunity!

"Not to worry, Mr. Cryder. You don't have to close your shop. I'll take good care of it."

"Let me think about it, Trevor."

As Mr. Cryder returned to his book work, Trevor's mind wandered back to his cousin. He had an idea that would make Skip think twice about messing with him again. But it all hinged on Mr. Cryder's decision.

A sudden thought hit him. *Don't do it, Trevor.*

Leave me alone, Lord. You took my dad when I needed him most, and I'm not ready to forgive you.

You promised Skip you'd be at ball practice, and you're not there.

Trevor thought about that. If he went to practice, he had all sorts of ways he could aggravate Skip. Then it occurred to him that Skip had such a winsome personality, that if he attended practice, he might start liking that man, and that would be disastrous. It would ruin his plan.

But for his plan to work, Trevor had to have unsupervised time at Mr. Cryder's motorcycle store. So he had to show his boss how responsible he was. He had to know how to run the entire business in less than ten days. Mr. Cryder had to feel confident in his reliability and trustworthiness.

So Trevor worked extra hard to learn everything he could, to always be respectful, and to sell at least one motorcycle all by himself.

With a sigh, Trevor pushed open the door to Mr. Cryder's motorcycle shop. It was a bright, sunny, Friday morning, the day of Karen's wedding. And Mr. Cryder had yet to ask him to mind the store for even part of the day.

I guess he decided to close it after all.

"Is that you, Trevor?" called Mr. Cryder from his office.

"Yes, sir."

"Good." Mr. Cryder joined him in the showroom. "After a lot of thought and careful consideration, I've decided to let you run things for me and lock up at six."

Trevor's eyes widened.

"There's a lot to do before a wedding, so even though Karen's wedding doesn't start until five, I'm gonna cut out of here about one. That means you'll be on your own for five hours. Can you handle it, or should I just close up at that time?"

"Oh, no, sir. I assure you. I can handle it. And I know how to close the sale on a motorcycle. I sold one yesterday."

"You sure did. And you did an excellent job. I was really proud of you." Mr. Cryder handed Trevor a key. "Here's my spare key. Don't lose it. And don't close early. Lock up exactly at six o'clock, and I'll see you on Monday morning."

Chapter 27

A Little Deception

Sitting around the kitchen table visiting with his mother, Aunt Rose, Robby, and Cassandra, Skip heard the roar of a motorcycle out front. Just then, Stephanie and Sandy ran into the kitchen looking for him.

"Skip, there's a guy on a motorcycle looking for you," said Stephanie.

"His name's Trevor," added Sandy.

Skip glanced over at his Aunt Rose, whose pleading look reminded him to handle her son with love and care.

"Thank you, girls." Rising to his feet, Skip headed for the front door, wondering how Trevor managed to locate him.

He pushed through the door and strolled out to the road, where Trevor sat straddling a Harley Davidson motorcycle. Stephanie and Sandy followed him.

"Hey, Trevor, how did you find my house?"

"Robby gave me your address. You want to go for a ride?"

"Where'd you get the bike?" asked Skip.

"I borrowed it from my boss. You like it?"

"Your boss loaned you his bike?" The thought stunned Skip. "You've only been working there a couple of weeks."

"That's true. So do you want to take a spin with me or not?"

"I thought you were mad at me."

"I've just been bothered by something lately. Get on. I'll tell you about it later."

Trevor was wearing a helmet and he handed one to Skip. Skip slowly took it, eyeing the motorcycle. It was a big one, and there was no protection. He could be putting his life into the hands of a reckless hot rodder by climbing on. And since Trevor had been so standoffish toward him lately, he wondered about the devious motive that lay behind his unexpected offer.

"What's the matter, Skip? Don't tell me you've never ridden on a motorcycle before."

He hadn't, and he didn't want his first experience to be a negative one. Then he thought of his Aunt Rose. If he could do anything to get through to Trevor and make a positive impact on his life, he'd do it. And he had no idea what he could accomplish with one little motorcycle ride, so he reluctantly strapped on the helmet.

"There's nothing to it. Just remember to lean with the bike. The key is to relax."

"Okay." Skip climbed on to the back of the bike and waved at his little sisters as they rode away. It would be dark soon, but he expected to be home by then. Trevor headed for the mountains.

"Hey, where are we going?" yelled Skip. He would have jumped off the bike at the first red light and hiked home, but as it happened, Trevor caught every light green on his way out of town. Reaching the foot of the mountains, he started up the two-lane road.

"Trevor, where are we going?" hollered Skip above the roar of the wind. "It's late, and I need to get home."

Trevor ignored him. As the trail became increasingly narrow and winding, Trevor increased his speed.

"Slow down," yelled Skip. "Trevor, slow down before you take us both over the edge of that cliff." Holding on tightly, he closed his eyes as his cousin practically laid down the bike to make the corners.

Skip breathed a prayer for safety. He knew that if God didn't protect him, he would join his father tonight. The remainder of the ride, he endured with his eyes closed. Suddenly the bike screeched to a halt. Trembling all over, Skip scrambled off the motorcycle.

Trevor glared at him. "I hope you enjoyed the ride, Shaughnessy."

Skip raised an eyebrow.

"You deceived me. You knew all the time that we were cousins. Well, good luck finding your way home, Cuz."

Trevor took off on the motorcycle, stranding Skip out in the middle of nowhere. Skip unstrapped the helmet and slowly removed it. With pursed lips, he shook his head and watched the motorcycle disappear from view.

"Trevor, you have a lot of growing up to do."

Removing his dark glasses, he slid them into his pocket. As darkness settled around him, he slowly started down the long, winding mountain road, thankful for a full moon. Now, if he only had a way to call home.

Chapter 28

A Cry for Help

Although Johnny still needed crutches, he was finally back at work. Assigned light duty at the station, he worked evenings in the control room. He answered the phone, manned the radio, took reports from walk-ins, and helped the night clerk with administrative details.

A tall, muscular man wearing a tuxedo bounded in, reporting that his motorcycle had been stolen. He suspected his new employee.

Johnny pulled out a blank report. "What's your name? Do you have some ID?"

"Name? Oh, I'm sorry. I'm just so upset. My name is Adam Cryder." With a sigh, he handed Johnny his driver's license.

"Mr. Cryder, what's the name of the employee you suspect?"

"Trevor Thompson."

Johnny's eyes widened. *Oh, no.*

Adam ran his fingers through his hair. "During my daughter's wedding, I remembered something I'd forgotten at my store, so after everything was over, I ran by to pick it up. I noticed the Harley Davidson was gone, so I looked for the paperwork that would indicate Trevor had made a sale, but there was no paperwork."

Johnny took down the report and promised to call when they had any information. As soon as Mr. Cryder left the station, Johnny snatched up the phone and dialed Skip's number to find out if this could be the same Trevor Thompson who should have been coming to baseball practice.

Erin answered. "I'm sorry, Johnny. Skip's not here. The girls told me that he went for a ride on a motorcycle."

"When was this?"

"An hour ago, and I'm getting worried. He should have been home by now."

"Erin, this is extremely important. Do you know who he was with?"

"He was with his cousin, Trevor Thompson."

"Okay. When he gets home, have him call the station immediately. I need to talk to him."

"Sure will, Johnny."

But when one hour lapsed into two, Erin called the station to inform them that Skip had not yet returned home.

Skip hiked down the long, narrow road, swinging the motorcycle helmet by the strap. He was tempted to leave it. It was getting heavy, and he was tired. But every time he started to put it down, he remembered that it was borrowed, and it had to be returned. An hour into his walk, Skip spied a long stick on the side of the roadway.

"Just what I need – a walking stick." He snatched it up without even breaking his stride. As he strode down the winding mountain road, he thought he heard a faint voice in the distance. Skip stopped to listen, but he didn't hear anything.

Must have been the wind. With a yawn, he continued the downward trek.

Skip strained to read his watch. It was after eleven. At this rate, he would be walking all night. Again he heard a distant call for help. Stopping suddenly, he strained to listen.

"Help," called a faint, hoarse voice. "Somebody, please help me."

Skip heard it clearly that time. With a raised eyebrow, he glanced around. He saw nothing but a narrow, two-lane highway and a rough slope down the mountainside. Strolling to the edge, he peered over. All he saw was blackness. Skip resumed his walk.

"Help!" came the call again. "Help me. Please." The voice grew louder and Skip was able to localize it. It was coming from up ahead, so he followed the sound of his cousin's voice right to the edge.

"Help. I'm stuck and can't get free. Lord Jesus, if You get me out of this mess, I'll serve You from now on."

Skip burst into laughter.

"Skip, are you up there?"

Sitting down on the edge of the slope, Skip felt the cool breeze sift through his hair. He set down his walking stick and the helmet, listening with amusement to Trevor struggle right beneath him.

"Skip, are you there? Can you hear me?" called Trevor. "Talk to me, will you?"

Skip yawned. He gazed up at the stars in silence.

Trevor let out a big sigh. "Skip?" His voice quivered and Skip detected a note of desperation. "Answer me."

Examining the steep slope from where he sat, Skip rolled to his stomach and started the dangerous climb down to his cousin. Not that Trevor deserved his help, for he didn't. But then, Skip knew that he didn't deserve the mercy God had extended on his behalf when he accepted Jesus as his Savior.

And since Jesus forgives me over and over again, I should also forgive Trevor.

"Skip, is that you?" Trevor made no effort to hide the tremor in his voice. "Skip? Please talk to me."

Since Trevor kept talking, Skip had no difficulty zeroing in on his location. He moved slowly, feeling his way down the steep, grassy slope. As he climbed down toward his cousin, he stepped on a large tree, growing crooked on the mountainside. Planting both feet firmly on the side of the tree, Skip sat down on it, leaning back against the slope.

"Trevor, where are you?"

"Skip? Oh, thank God, you found me. I thought you'd never get here. I'm stuck. One of the branches from this huge tree caught me by the back of the belt, and I can't get loose."

"And what makes you think I'd risk my neck to rescue you?"

"Because you're my cousin."

"What does that have to do with anything? It didn't do me any good when you stranded me atop this mountain."

"But isn't that why you bailed me out of jail?"

"Not hardly. From the looks of things, I should have left you there. Are you hurt anywhere?"

"Yeah, I hurt my arm and I think my leg is broken."

"What happened?" asked Skip.

"I was coming down the hill fast and hit an oil slick in the middle of a turn. I lost control of the bike and went over the edge. Lucky for me this tree was here."

"Lucky, huh? Trevor, you're living on borrowed time. Almighty God kept that bike from coming down on top of you. And He made sure that tree limb snagged your britches. What else does He have to do to you before you'll listen to Him? I heard you tell Him that if He got you out of this mess, you'd serve Him. Did you mean it?"

"I guess so. I don't know."

"I'll take that as a 'no.' Well, hold on, and don't panic. I'm coming down, so stay still. I don't know what's below us, and I don't want to find out the hard way."

Lord, I can't leave him in this predicament, and I have no way to call for help. So I'm trusting You to strengthen and guide me on my rescue attempt.

Descending slowly, Skip felt his way down to his cousin. Trevor encircled a protruding rock with one arm, while Skip kept a firm grip on an overhanging branch from the gigantic tree he'd been sitting on.

"Hold on tight." Skip clasped the tree branch that had snagged Trevor's belt. He attempted to snap it off, but it was too sturdy. Of course, the strength of the branch is what had kept Trevor from falling to his death. Grasping the heavy branch just below his belt, Skip attempted to shove it downward, but due to his precarious position on the mountainside, he couldn't get the leverage he needed to free Trevor's belt from the clutches of the large branch.

Skip breathed a heavy sigh. He was starting to feel fatigued from hanging on for dear life. If his grip slipped, he'd fall to his death, and Trevor would probably die in that tree. The chances of someone stopping their vehicle at this spot on the mountain and happening to see or hear him calling for help was almost nonexistent.

Lord, I need help. I can't do this by myself, and I have no desire to sacrifice my life trying. "Trevor, I need to climb back up to rest."

Trevor started to whine. "No, Skip, don't leave me. Please." Without thinking, he grabbed Skip.

"No. Let go of me," cried Skip. "Before you make me fall."

Trevor clung to him. *"Don't leave me here!"*

Chapter 29

The Long Trek Home

With Trevor hanging onto him, Skip tightened his grip on the tree branch to keep from sliding down the mountainside. "Knock it off, and let go of me before you make us both fall."

"Skip, I'm scared."

"Grow up, Trevor. You got yourself into this mess and there's no way you'll get out of it by yourself. Now, you listen to me and do exactly as I tell you, or I will leave you in this tree. *Let go of me.*"

Trevor released him.

Skip breathed a sigh of relief, but he was still no closer to freeing Trevor than before he found him. *Lord, where do I even begin?*

With the problem.

With the problem? thought Skip. *But the problem is the tree branch.*

Just then it hit him what God was trying to tell him. *No. The problem is his belt.*

"Okay, Trevor, hang on for all your worth. God's given me the solution, and in a minute that tree branch will no longer be supporting you. And you'll need a good grip so you don't fall."

"I think I'm ready."

Reaching under his cousin, Skip unbuckled his belt. The instant he did, Trevor's weight against the tree branch yanked his belt out of the belt loops and it released him suddenly.

Trevor gasped and clung to that rock for life.

"That was the easy part," said Skip. "It's a long, hard climb to the top."

The slope was steep, but it had enough embedded rocks and vegetation to provide some natural footholds.

Skip climbed up a couple of feet. Reaching down, he grabbed Trevor by the back of the shirt and hauled him up. Trevor struggled to climb, but the pain from his leg was so intense he couldn't put any weight on it.

"I can't do it, Skip."

"You'd better do it because the alternative is worse. And how am I going to explain to your mother how you killed yourself?"

Trevor groaned. "But my leg hurts tremendously, and I can barely climb with only one arm."

"I don't care. Keep climbing."

Every couple of feet, Skip stopped to drag his cousin up beside him. By the time they reached the top, it was almost one o'clock in the morning, and the boys collapsed alongside the road to rest.

Skip didn't rest long. They still had a long walk ahead of them, and he had to get home. Sitting up, he gazed down at Trevor. "Now, where are you hurt?"

"I think I broke my leg because I can't walk. We'll have to wait here until somebody comes."

"You're crazy if you think I'm just going to sit here and wait for a Good Samaritan to rescue us. It could be two or three days before a car comes through here."

Trevor sat up. "What do you expect me to do? I can't walk." With his belt dangling through one belt loop by the buckle, he re-threaded it through the belt loops.

"You'll have to walk. We've got to get back to town." Skip examined Trevor's leg. "It's swollen."

"It's broken," yelled Trevor, buckling his belt. "And I told you that I can't walk. Boy, are you dense."

Skip sighed and looked toward Heaven. *So much for gratitude, Lord.* "Are you through being nasty?" he asked Trevor.

"No, I have more to say."

"Fine, but I'm not going to be here to hear it." Skip stood up and walked away.

"Hey, where are you going?"

"Home. I'll send a police car after you." With a yawn, Skip strolled down the highway.

"No, no, don't leave me."

He was so tired of Trevor's whining.

"Skip, please."

If he kept on going, he would eventually be out of ear shot.

"I'm sorry for what I said, but I can't put any weight on my leg."

And once he was out of ear shot, he'd enjoy a nice quiet walk down the mountain without listening to Trevor's constant moaning and groaning. No more babysitting.

"Skiiiip!"

Skip glanced behind him.

No! No! Don't look back. It's a mistake.

Too late. Skip saw the shadow of his cousin waving at him, and he immediately thought of his Aunt Rose. How could he explain to her that he abandoned her son while Trevor begged for help?

Well, I did help him. Otherwise, he'd still be caught in that tree.

Standing in the middle of the road, Skip slid his hands into his pockets and studied his cousin.

"Trevor, I'm going home."

"Take me with you."

"What? I thought you couldn't walk, so you were going to wait here until someone came to rescue you."

"I changed my mind."

Skip strolled back to his cousin. Picking up his walking stick, which he'd left lying on the ground, he examined it. "First thing we must do is splint your leg. But this stick is too long. We'll have to cut it in two."

Skip pulled out his pocketknife and started sawing on the stick. It seemed to take forever, but he finally cut enough of a gash to break it in two pieces. Clipping his glasses to the neck of his undershirt, he slipped off his shirt and cut it into strips. Trevor watched as his cousin positioned the stick at the back of his leg and securely tied it in place with the strips of cloth.

"Aah!" Trevor cried out in pain.

Skip heaved a frustrated sigh. If Trevor's leg was broken, then he was in a lot of pain, so Skip tried to be patient, but his patience was growing extremely thin. It didn't help that he had been up for almost twenty-four hours.

Trevor had set him up and then stranded him. Skip had to rescue him from the dangerous predicament he'd gotten himself into. And after all that, Trevor's only expression of gratitude was insolence and name-calling. So it wouldn't take much for him to walk away and leave his belligerent cousin on his own.

"There." Skip tightened the last knot and handed Trevor the left over piece of his walking stick. "Use this like a cane, and you should be able to keep a lot of your weight off this leg. Now let's see if you can stand."

Ducking under Trevor's left arm, Skip supported him and lifted him to his feet.

"Aah!" Trevor grimaced and drew in a sharp breath.

"Well?" asked Skip.

With a pained look, his cousin nodded, and the boys started their long trek down the mountain trail back to town.

"Okay, Trevor, now tell me the truth. Where'd you get the motorcycle?"

"I told you the truth. I borrowed it from my boss, but without his knowledge or permission. It's probably been reported stolen by now. I intended to return it, Skip. You've got to believe me."

"I do, but will your boss?"

"Boy, I hope so or I'm on my way to prison. There's no way I can return it now. Skip, can you use your authority as a police officer to get me out of this mess?"

Skip laughed. "You're joking, right? I couldn't even use my authority as a police officer to steer you in the right direction. You were determined to do what you wanted regardless of what I said or did."

Trevor sighed. "I guess my goose is cooked. My mom warned me that if I kept running from God, He might do something drastic to get my attention. I know I'm going to jail for this."

Skip yawned constantly, shivering in the cool night air as he helped his cousin down the never-ending road.

"You all right?" Trevor asked him.

"No. I'm exhausted. I'm freezing. I'm so hungry I have a headache. But that's what you wanted, right?"

"I'm ashamed to admit that I did. I'm sorry I ever felt that way. I'm sorry for getting you into this mess. And I'm sorry for my bad attitude."

Skip looked at Trevor. His apologies were genuine.

"That lady was right," said Trevor.

"What lady?"

"The one I stole the apples from. She said you'd been a real friend to me and that I should appreciate you. What makes you so different?"

"I've given my life to Jesus."

"Well, I know Jesus as my Savior."

"You think He's happy with your behavior?"

"No."

"You've been running from Him, like Jonah did. Turn your life over to Him, Trev. Let Him guide you day by day. Be in the house of God every chance you get. Pray earnestly and spend quality time in your Bible every day. God doesn't just want to save you. He wants to *change* you."

"I appreciate you, Skip. Thanks for being there when I didn't even know that I needed someone. I think I'd like to be a cop like you, but it's too late now. I'm going to be charged with grand theft auto."

"I have an idea, but it will require some humbling on your part."

"Anything's better than prison."

"Of course, it's not guaranteed to work, but right now you have nothing to lose. Go to your mom and tell her your situation. Ask her for a loan to replace the motorcycle."

"A loan?"

"Yes, a loan. It'll do you good to have to pay it back. Then, go to your boss and tell him the entire truth, offering to replace his bike if he doesn't press charges."

"That will require some humbling."

"It's either that or prison."

"It's probably prison anyway. My mother would never give me a loan after everything I've done. Besides that, I haven't been able to get a hold of her. I've called home a couple of times since I've been here. I just get the recorder."

"She's been staying at my house. And I think she'll give you a loan if you ask."

"She's at your house? No wonder Robby didn't want to move back in with me. I wonder why he hasn't said anything."

"We asked him not to. You're welcome to stay with us, if you'd like. Your mother has been worried sick about you."

The boys dragged slowly down the hill. It was almost four o'clock in the morning, and Skip's eyes burned with fatigue. But they had to keep going. They had to get back to town. The big game against Alcova was at noon, and Skip was determined not to miss it.

Chapter 30

The Search Continues

Erin paced the floor, constantly glancing at the clock. Cassandra peeked out the window every time she heard a car, and Rose sat on the couch wringing her hands. Robby had fallen asleep on the living room floor.

"Oh, Skip, where are you?" Cassandra peeked through the curtains again, but it was pitch dark outside.

The ladies had prayed for them all evening and well into the night. Now there was nothing to do but wait.

By the time the police department had organized a search, it was almost eleven o'clock. Since the search involved one of their own, they called in every off-duty officer. Practically every police officer in town was out looking for Skip and Trevor.

At the onset of the search, Robby had shown Jesse where his brother slept at night, so the police put a twenty-four hour surveillance on the basement door. Pictures of the missing boys and a snap shot of the motorcycle were broadcast on the local news stations, requesting anyone who had seen them to call the police department. But no one called.

Leaning against the police car, his arms and legs both crossed, Jesse yawned and rubbed his eyes. They'd been searching all night. "Boy, am I tired. I was ready for bed hours ago."

"What time is it?" asked Kevin.

Jesse looked at his wristwatch, staring at it, trying to bring it into focus. "Um ..." He squinted. "Almost five thirty."

"With all the news programs broadcasting their pictures, you'd think that someone would have seen them somewhere. I find it unusual that no one has called – not one person. It's like they just vanished."

Jesse caught his breath. He stood up straight and looked toward the mountains. "Unless they headed out of town."

"Now why on earth would Skip leave town without telling anyone, especially with the big game coming up?"

"Maybe he didn't go willingly," said Jesse. "We've searched the town thoroughly. Let's grab a bite to eat and head for the mountains."

Skip and Trevor had been walking for hours. Worse yet, Trevor was moving so slowly they couldn't have gone more than two or three miles. Skip was hungry and thirsty, cold and tired. But he was downright exhausted from Trevor leaning on him so heavily.

"Skip, can't we rest for a minute? I'm so tired. My leg hurts so bad. I have to get off of it for awhile."

"All right. You got five minutes." Skip helped Trevor down to the ground, then dropped beside him. "Look, it's getting lighter. In less than an hour, the sun will be coming up. Have you ever seen a sunrise before?"

Trevor shook his head.

"You'll see one today." With a yawn, Skip lay back on the side of the road and rested his eyes. "They're absolutely gorgeous."

Trevor studied Skip, who seemed to rest comfortably and peacefully. But his leg hurt so badly, he couldn't get comfortable no matter what he did. Walking easily magnified the pain by ten, so he was not in a hurry to resume their hike down the long, winding mountain road. And he didn't care about that dumb ballgame. All he cared about right now was relieving the pain.

Unfortunately, his five-minute rest time was up ten minutes ago, and Skip still wasn't stirring.

"Skip?" Trevor started to shake him. *Wait a minute. He's sound asleep. As long as he's sleeping, I can sit here and keep my weight off of my leg.*

Then it occurred to him, he'd eventually have to walk down this mountain to get medical aid because in all the time they'd been there, not one car had passed them from either direction. He and Skip had no food or water with them. And the only One who knew where they were was God.

Tears burned his eyes as he looked over at Skip, who was in this predicament because he had cared enough to get involved with Trevor. And despite his effort to hurt Skip, he witnessed the hand of God protecting his cousin.

Folding his hands and bowing his head, Trevor reverently talked to God. "Lord, I'm sorry for my attitude and my actions. I've caused my mother and brother great hurt. And you only protected me last night because of Skip."

Trevor choked back tears as he considered all that Skip had gone through because of him. "He didn't deserve any of this. Lord, I can hardly walk. There's no way we'll get home in time for that game if we have to walk it. And that game means a lot to Skip. I doubt that anyone is missing me, but they've got to be looking for him. Send someone up this mountain trail."

A peace that he'd never felt before settled in his heart. When he looked up from praying, he caught sight of the sunrise. Trevor stared toward the eastern sky in fascination as the brilliant sunlight peeked over the horizon, chasing away the darkness.

"Oh, man, is that gorgeous."

Jesse was glad that Kevin was driving because he was about to fall asleep. They were on a two-lane, black topped mountain road. To their right was the mountain. To their left was the unforgiving drop-off if one veered too close to the edge.

Jesse yawned and lowered his window. Hopefully, the cool breeze would keep him awake. "You don't suppose they went over the edge on the motorcycle, do you?"

"I certainly hope not."

The patrol car crawled along at a measly thirty miles per hour. He knew that Kevin wanted to be able to stop suddenly if they found something worth investigating or if they came across Skip or Trevor hiking down the road toward home. There was no safe place to walk along the road, and they didn't want to accidentally run over anyone.

They drove higher and higher into the mountains looking for any indication that Skip or Trevor had even been there.

Jesse sighed. "Well, I guess it was a good thought."

"Hey, we haven't reached the top yet. We could still come across them."

"You think we will?"

Kevin glanced at him and back at the road. "Not really. Is there any place to turn around so we can head back to town?"

"No, this stretch of road is pretty narrow. There is a turn-around plateau, but it's still quite a ways up there, so we're stuck making the drive."

"I was afraid you'd say that."

Kevin continued on up the mountain for another ten miles. "How much farther to that plateau?"

"I don't know. I don't think it's much farther."

Circling the mountain on their upward climb, they were no longer looking for Skip or Trevor. They were just looking for the turn-around spot that was big enough for them to make a u-turn and start back down the mountain. Kevin suddenly hit the brake pedal, jarring Jesse awake.

"What is it? What happened?" Jesse jerked upright and glanced around frantically. His eyes zeroed in on a guy lying on the side of the road. "Skip." His heart nearly stopped as he jumped from the vehicle. The officers bolted to Skip and dropped to their knees at his side.

"Skip!"

At the sound of his name, Skip's eyes fluttered open and he looked up at them. "Kevin, Jesse. Boy, am I glad to see you guys."

"Are you hurt anywhere?" asked Kevin. "Can you sit up?"

Skip slowly sat up and rubbed his eyes. "I'm okay. We just stopped to rest, and I guess I fell asleep."

"Skip, what happened?" asked Jesse. "The entire police department is looking for you."

"Well um ..." Skip glanced from Trevor to Kevin and back to Jesse. "We ran into some unexpected problems on our motorcycle ride. But I'm okay, just ..." Skip glanced down at his clothes and winced. "... dirty."

Kevin laughed. "Well, hey, now you look normal."

"Yeah." Skip got to his feet and dusted off his clothes the best he could.

Seeing Trevor's condition, Jesse and Kevin gently lifted him and carried him to the car, helping him into the back seat. Skip crawled in beside him.

Kevin and Jesse jumped into the front seat of the car and took off. Jesse snatched up the radio mic, informing dispatch that they'd found Skip and Trevor stranded on a deserted mountain road and that they were transporting the boys to the hospital.

Kevin sighed as they drove up further and further into the mountains. Spotting the abandoned motorcycle helmet, he stopped the car, and Jesse jumped out to retrieve it. He gasped when he saw the motorcycle lying at the bottom of the steep slope in a mangled heap. Jumping back into the car, they continued up the narrow road. At last they reached the small plateau where Kevin turned the car around.

The loud jangle of the telephone woke Cassandra around 7:15. Bouncing to her feet, she snatched up the receiver before it woke everyone else, but she needn't have hurried. Rose and Erin were at her side in seconds.

"Hello?"

"Cassandra, this is Captain Kramer. We've found Skip, and he's all right."

"What about Trevor?"

"Yeah, Trevor was with him. It looks like he may have a broken leg. Kevin and Jesse are transporting them to the hospital."

"Thanks, Captain." Cassandra hung up and turned to the others with a big grin that said it all.

"They found them both?" asked Rose.

"Yes, Skip's in good shape, but Trevor may have a broken leg. They're on their way to the hospital now."

The living room became a bustle of activity as the ladies prepared to go to the hospital.

"Who's staying with the girls?" asked Cassandra. "Could Robby babysit?"

Shaking her head, Erin grabbed the phone and punched in a number from memory. "I'll ask Ruth if she can come over. Robby will want to go."

Robby rubbed his eyes and sat up. "Go where?"

"The hospital. The police found Skip and Trevor, and they're on the way there right now."

Chapter 31

A Family Reunion

By the time they reached the hospital, it was almost eight o'clock. Disappointment washed over Cassandra when she realized that Skip wasn't there yet. Anxious to see them the instant they arrived, the family all stood outside at the emergency entrance waiting for the police car. When the squad car pulled in, Cassandra hurried toward the back door.

Leaping from the car, Jesse and Kevin gently redirected Skip's anxious family out of the way and cleared a path for the emergency personnel, who wheeled gurneys to either side of the car. They yanked open both rear doors simultaneously, and the Emergency Department technicians lifted the sleeping boys from the car.

Trevor cried out in pain as they hoisted him onto a gurney and wheeled him into Emergency. Rose and Robby followed them in.

Skip awoke with a start. "No! I'm gonna fall!" Fighting the Emergency personnel, he kicked and struggled.

"Whoa, son, take it easy. You're all right." Holding him tightly, they restrained him.

Opening his eyes, Skip stopped struggling. "Oh, I'm sorry. I was dreaming."

Despite his protests, they set him on a gurney and wheeled him into Emergency.

Cassandra and Erin followed him into treatment room four where they lifted him onto the bed. His eyes dropped shut again. Standing on either side of his bed, his wife and mother gently touched him.

"Skip, what happened?" asked Cassandra.

"It's a long story. I'll tell you later."

Trevor groaned in pain as he waited for the doctor.

Robby leaned on the railing of his bed and grasped his hand. "Trev, did you really steal a motorcycle?"

"I intended to return it, but now I can't. Robby, I owe you an apology for the way I've been behaving. Will you forgive me?"

Robby raised an eyebrow. Trevor could tell that was not something Robby ever expected to hear from him.

"Yeah, I forgive you."

"Where's Mom? Did she come with you?"

"She's out in the waiting room. She thinks you don't want to see her."

"I do. Would you get her for me?"

Robby left the room to fetch his mother. A moment later, Rose entered treatment room two and stepped over to his bed. She grasped the railing and looked into her son's eyes. Seeing that Robby didn't follow her back in, Trevor assumed that his brother was giving them an opportunity to talk in private, and he appreciated that.

Trevor placed his hand on top of his mother's. "Mom, I'm sorry for my behavior. Will you forgive me?"

Rose smiled at him. "Of course, I forgive you. Trevor, did you steal that motorcycle?"

"I guess, I did. I'm so sorry, Mom. I didn't mean to steal it. I borrowed it without permission, and now I can't return it. Would you consider...?" Trevor swallowed hard and collected all his courage. "I need to replace Mr. Cryder's bike, and I won't be able to do that where I'm going. Just a loan, Mom. I'll pay back every cent, with interest."

"But, Trevor, why do you want to replace it if you'll be paying for it by serving jail time?"

"Because I'm a child of God, and I know that God would have me replace it."

"Trevor, have you given any thought to what you want to do with your life?"

"Yeah, I have, but it's too late now. Will you give me the loan, Mom? As soon as I'm able, I'll get a good job and pay you back."

"My goodness. What's changed you?"

Trevor sighed and glanced away. "It's a long story, Mom. So may I have the loan?"

"I can't give you a loan, but because I love you, I will give you the money."

Trevor paused, considering what his mother had just said. "Thanks, Mom, but I can't take it. I believe God wants me to pay for it myself."

With a grin, Rose grasped his hand. "You really have matured. Yes, you may have the loan."

The doctor stepped into the room, washed his hands, and examined Trevor before sending him to radiology.

After taking Skip and Trevor to the hospital, Jesse and Kevin returned to the station and clocked out. Jesse had been up for over twenty-four hours and he desperately needed some sleep. But the big game was only three hours away, and he wanted to check on Skip, so he headed to the hospital.

When he located Skip in the ED, Cassandra and Erin were with him, and Skip was sound asleep on the bed. Since Skip hadn't told them anything, Jesse briefed them on what little he knew.

While he was telling them that the motorcycle went over the cliff, the doctor walked in. He washed his hands and woke Skip to question and examine him.

"Skip, you look real good. The nurse will be in with the discharge paperwork and you can get out of here."

"That's great!" cried Jesse. "Especially after he went over the cliff on a motorcycle."

The doctor raised an eyebrow. "Not this boy. There's no evidence – not one mark to indicate he took a spill."

"Hey, Skip, tell the doctor that you and Trevor went over the edge with that bike."

Skip rubbed the sleep from his eyes and sat up. "Not me. Just Trevor."

Visiting with his mom and brother while waiting for the results of the x-ray, Trevor started to get anxious about facing Mr. Cryder. But before he had too much time to linger on his concerns, the doctor returned to his room with a technician wheeling a cart.

"It's definitely broken," said the doctor. "We'll need to splint it for now, which will stabilize it while the swelling goes down. Then in a couple of days, you'll need to see an orthopedic specialist to cast it. We'll set you up with an appointment for Tuesday morning. In the meantime, stay off of your leg as much as possible and keep it on ice."

The doctor left and the technician prepared to splint Trevor's leg.

With his discharge paperwork in hand, Skip hopped off the table. It was nine thirty and Jesse had already left, promising to meet him at the ballpark.

"Well, I had a nice little nap. Hopefully that'll get me through the game. Let's go find out what's going on with Trevor."

Erin and Cassandra followed Skip to treatment room two where they located Trevor and his family. The technician was in the process of splinting Trevor's leg.

"You think you'll make it to the ballgame?" asked Skip.

The technician frowned. "He'd better not go anywhere but home so he can prop and ice this leg."

Trevor glanced at the technician and then looked at Skip. "I can't go to the game. I need to face my boss and turn myself in."

"You want me to go with you?"

"Thanks, Skip, but this is something I have to do by myself."

"Okay, pal." Skip grasped his hand. "Good luck."

"Pray for me. I'm going to need it."

"You bet." Skip looked at his mom. "Wait! How are they getting home if we take the car?"

"We brought both cars so we all didn't have to cram into one. And it's a good thing we did."

"Robby, why don't you go home with Skip," said Rose. "I'll stay with Trevor."

Robby bounded to his feet. "Great. Let's go. I'm hungry."

As soon as Skip entered the house, his little sisters bulldozed him over and piled on top of him, hugging him constantly and inundating him with kisses. Ordinarily, he could slide out from under them and send them off to play, but this morning he was too tired to resist their affection.

"We missed you, Skip," said Suzi, hugging his neck and resting her head on his shoulder.

"Are you all right?" asked Stephanie. "I worried about you all night."

"All night?" echoed Skip. "Weren't you sleeping?"

"Well, sometimes I woke up long enough to worry."

Skip laughed. "I see."

"Okay, girls. Let your brother up so he can eat and get ready for his ballgame," said Erin.

As the girls crawled off Skip, he rose to his feet. "Thanks, Mom."

Skip hurried to shower and change into his ball uniform. It felt good to be clean again, dressed in a clean ball uniform, but his growling stomach reminded him that he hadn't eaten since dinner last night. Hurrying downstairs into the kitchen, Skip sat beside Robby, who was also dressed for the ballgame. Cassandra and Erin had prepared a big breakfast for them all and were just sitting down to eat.

After breakfast, Skip and Robby engaged the girls in a game of Go Fish. Skip needed something to keep him awake. He was afraid that if he fell asleep, he'd sleep through the ballgame, so he had no intentions of lying down.

Trevor thought he'd never get through at the hospital, not that he was in a hurry to confront his boss. He dreaded owning up to his reckless decision, but that's what he had to do, and he knew it.

Hobbling out the door on crutches, he followed his mother to her rental car. His leg throbbed so badly that he wished he could just go home and lie down. Instead they were headed for the motorcycle store where he had worked.

With great difficulty, Trevor maneuvered himself into the front passenger seat. He could hardly keep his eyes open, but he had to give his mom directions to the store. She didn't know her way around town. When they reached the motorcycle shop, Rose turned into the small parking lot located in the back. She pulled her checkbook from her purse, tore out a check, and handed it to Trevor.

"You talk to your former employer about the replacement cost of his bike. Write out this check for the full amount, including tax. Then bring it to me, and I'll sign it."

"Thanks, Mom. I appreciate this." Folding the check, he slipped it into his shirt pocket. Trevor struggled onto his crutches and closed the car door. He hobbled into the store and over to the counter.

"Well, I didn't expect to see you here again," said Mr. Cryder. "I'm calling the police."

"Before you do, may I say something?"

With the cordless phone in his hand, Mr. Cryder said, "Go ahead."

"I'm sorry for taking your motorcycle without permission. I know that's stealing, but I fully intended to return it."

"Okay, you had your say." Mr. Cryder phoned the police.

As soon as he hung up, Trevor continued. "I wrecked your bike and would like to replace it."

"I'm sorry, Trevor. It will take you years to work off that debt, and you're obviously not trustworthy."

"I'm borrowing the money, so I can pay you in full now. How much would it cost me to purchase a Harley Davidson motorcycle just like yours, tax and all?"

"Hm, let me see." Mr. Cryder pulled out a calculator and started tapping in some figures, calculating the cost of a brand new motorcycle just like his. He jotted the figure on a piece of paper and slid it over to Trevor.

Trevor pulled the check from his pocket and opened it up to write on it.

"Let me see that." Mr. Cryder snatched the check away from him and looked at it. "Now, Trevor, you know I don't take out-of-state checks."

"Mr. Cryder, this is just one of many accounts in my mother's name which has more than a hundred thousand dollars in it. I'm borrowing the money from her. I assure you, the check is good." Taking the check from Mr. Cryder, Trevor filled it in and handed it back to him.

The front door opened and two police officers entered the building.

Trevor glanced at them and turned back to Mr. Cryder. "My mom is sitting in the red Ford out back. Take it out to her and she'll sign it." Without waiting for a reply, he hobbled toward the door on his crutches and left the store with the two officers.

Chapter 32

In Need of One Run

Adam studied the check. How could he go out there and have Mrs. Thompson sign it after sending her son to jail? He walked out into the bright sunlight, watching the police officers seat Trevor in the back seat of the police car and drive away.

Glancing from the check to the red Ford on the other side of the parking lot, Adam strolled toward the car, approaching the woman's open window. He handed her the check and started to walk away.

"Oh, wait, Mr. Cryder." She scribbled her signature and handed it back.

"Ma'am, can you afford this?"

"Yes, and a dozen more just like it. I was going to get Trevor a motorcycle for his birthday, but I guess he won't need it now. I'm sorry for the trouble he caused you, Mr. Cryder."

"Ma'am, you don't have to do this, ya know."

"I'm not. Trevor is. He feels he ought to replace your bike, and I agree. He took it without permission. He destroyed it. He is replacing it. This money is only a loan. He's going to pay me back."

Adam studied her face for a moment. "You look familiar. I know you from someplace."

"Do you remember Stephen Shaughnessy?"

"Of course. Who doesn't?"

"I'm his sister."

Adam snapped his fingers. "Stephanie Rose. Of course. And Trevor's your son?"

Rose smiled. "Yes. He's like a misguided missile. How I wish that Stephen were here to straighten him up."

Adam looked at the check he held in his hand and back to Rose. "Just like my boy. If it weren't for Steve, he'd probably be in prison today. Come on, Rose. Let's go get that boy out of jail. I'll drop the charges and give him another chance."

Shortly before eleven, Rose spun the car into the driveway. With a sigh, she cut the engine and looked at her son. "I am so glad that's over, and I'm thankful that you knew the way. I would have gotten lost."

"Mom, I appreciate you." Struggling to position his crutches as he climbed out of the car, Trevor hobbled through the front door.

Skip and Robby were getting ready to leave.

"Do I have time to clean up so I can go with you?" asked Trevor.

"Yeah, but you'll need to hurry," said Skip. "Or you'll make us late."

"Do you happen to have another baseball jersey?" asked Trevor.

"I do, but it has my name on it."

"I don't care." Trevor washed up and changed into Skip's extra jersey. As soon as he was ready, they headed out the door.

"Bye, Mom," called the boys.

"Hey, wait for me!" Cassandra raced after them.

Rose looked at Erin. "Grab the girls and let's go. I want to see the game. Robby is pitching."

When Trevor and the others arrived at the park, the rest of the team was already there.

Seeing him hobble toward the field on crutches, Damon trotted over to him. "What happened to you? And why are you wearing Skip's shirt? Where's yours?"

"It's a long story." Tottering into the dugout, Trevor plopped down on the bench to watch the game.

Since the Forest Valley boys were the home team, they trotted onto the field. Trevor stared into the field with bland enthusiasm. Even the excitement of the game couldn't capture his attention. At this moment, he had only one thing on his mind.

The ballplayers ran and yelled, stole bases, got pickled, and scored run after run. The game was like a see-saw as the lead bounced between the two teams.

Trevor's stare remained stagnant despite the exciting game and cheering spectators.

"You look tired," said Johnny. Setting his crutches down beside Trevor's, he dropped onto the bench beside him. "You want to talk about it?"

Trevor stared into the field. "I wish I were like Skip, but ..."

Skip signaled the boy on first to steal second, and away he went.

"Safe!" cried the umpire.

"I've been in so much trouble and ..." Trevor studied Skip, watching every move he made. "I don't think I could ever be that kind of Christian."

"Why not? Trevor, let me tell you something about Skip. He was headed for trouble before his dad died. So if there's anyone who can relate with you, it's Skip."

"What happened to change him?"

"Your Uncle Stephen, Skip's dad, greatly loved the Lord. He was Skip's hero. When he died, Skip was forced into a world of decisions and responsibilities. God made a man out of him in a hurry. He had just turned sixteen."

Trevor pondered Johnny's statement. Then he looked from Skip to Robby. Robby seemed to mature after their dad died, too. He took on the responsibility of ensuring that their mother was cared for. No wonder he insisted on writing her that note when they left LA. Trevor had thought that Robby relied on his mama way too much, but he was taking on the responsibility of caring for his widowed mother, even though he was still a minor. And that's what Skip did at age sixteen. And both of them had recently said to him, *Grow up, Trevor.*

"You know, Johnny. I didn't realize it until this morning, but Skip's my best friend. Best friends truly care about you, and they tell it like it is, even when you don't like what they have to say."

Johnny sighed. "I know. I had a best friend like that once. His name was Stephen Shaughnessy."

Trevor did a double take. "Skip's dad was your best friend?"

"Indeed, he was. And he bailed me out of trouble just like I bailed Skip out of trouble, and Skip bailed you out of trouble."

"Wow. I'll remember that when someone comes into my life who's headed for trouble. Hey, Johnny, I've been wondering. How did you get so banged up?"

"Do you remember a few weeks ago when you, Robby, and Damon were speeding through town and a police car was chasing you?"

"How did you know about that?"

"I was the one chasing you. A pickup truck ran a red light and broadsided me."

"Oh, Johnny, I'm really sorry. Does Robby know?"

"He's been with Skip, so I'd imagine he does."

Skip couldn't believe this game. Every time his boys jumped into the lead, Alcova took it away from them when they came to bat. So they went into the top of the ninth inning ahead by only one run. If they could just hold onto their lead for one more out, the game would be theirs. But Alcova had runners on first and third.

"Come on, Robby. Just one more out and the game's over. Don't let this guy score." Skip wasn't actually talking to Robby. He was just thinking aloud.

Robby threw the ball, and the batter cracked a line drive past the shortstop and into left field, allowing the runner on third to cross home plate. That brought the roaring crowd to their feet as Alcova tied the game for the fourth time. People were jumping off the bleachers, screaming and waving their arms. With the runner now on second, Skip paced anxiously as Robby went into his windup. One solid hit would bring the runner home and they'd lose the lead again. And with only half an inning left to play, they might not score in the ninth.

The ball flew across home plate, and the batter missed. The bat whistled by the ball again for strike two. Skip held his breath. They were one pitch away from ending the inning. And in the bottom of the ninth, they'd only need one run to win the game.

Robby went into his wind up and threw the ball right down the center. The batter swung and the loud crack of the ball hitting the bat momentarily silenced the crowd. A line drive ripped through the air toward the second baseman. Diving for it, Robby snagged it out of midair and tumbled to the ground, rolling. As he sat up, he held up his glove, revealing that he had not dropped the ball.

Moving into the bottom of the ninth inning, the teams once again changed sides. And all they needed to win the game was one run.

"Chris, you're up to bat," said Skip. "Go hit us a home run." During practice, Chris had proven that he was a good batter, but he'd yet to get a base hit during the game.

"I'll try, but I'm not doing so well, coach."

"Whoa." Skip grabbed him before he left the dugout. "You're one of our best hitters."

"I'm 0 for 3."

"That just means that you're due a hit. Now go show your parents what you learned all those weeks of baseball practice."

"Yes, sir."

Skip watched as Chris took a solid batting stance, the best he'd done all game. The pitcher threw the ball and Chris came up under it with a solid swing that sent it sailing toward the fence. The Alcova outfielders turned around to chase it, but it dropped right outside the fence.

Chris completed his jog around the bases while Skip's boys emptied the dugout, whooping and hollering. The final score was nine to eight.

Chapter 33

Just Like Stephen

Skip strolled over to the dugout of the opposing team, shaking hands with the coach. "Your boys played an incredible game. You must be very proud of them."

"Thank you. I am."

As the crowd began to thin, Skip waved at Jesse. "Go home and get some sleep."

"I plan to. See you Monday morning."

Joining Skip, Cassandra looped her arm through his and escorted him back to the car. "That was an exciting game, Skip. You must be exhausted. I'll get the car door for you this time." Cassandra opened the driver's door for him.

Skip kissed her. "Thanks, Cassie. I'm so tired, I'm happy to accept."

Skip and Cassandra slid into the car and waited. A few minutes later, Robby opened the door for his brother and helped him into the car. Skip could tell that Trevor was in a lot of pain. He needed to go home and get off that leg.

Scrambling into the car beside his brother, Robby declared, "Wasn't that a great game! I think that was the best game I've ever pitched. I'll bet Mom loved it."

"Mom wasn't at the game," said Trevor.

"Sure she was. Mom's never missed one of my games. Why would she start now?"

Skip glanced at Robby's bubbly expression through his rear view mirror. *I wish I could say that about my mom. She's hardly been to a game since Stephanie was born.*

Skip pulled into the driveway and dragged himself out of the car. Cassandra and Robby helped Trevor from the car and guided him into the house. Wearily trailing them through the front door, Skip stopped just inside the door.

His four little sisters lay sprawled in front of the television. None of them ran to greet him this afternoon, which was probably a good thing, because if they knocked him down today, he might just fall asleep on the floor.

"Robby, you pitched a great game." Rose embraced him. "I'll bet you're hungry."

"Starved! When's lunch?" Without waiting for a reply, Robby trotted up the stairs.

Aunt Rose did go to the game, thought Skip. He looked around for Cassandra. She was trying to make Trevor comfortable on the sofa.

"I'll bring you a couple of pillows so you can prop your leg. And I'll bring you an ice pack to help reduce the swelling? Do you need some aspirin to ease the pain?"

It seemed strange to Skip to suddenly feel invisible in his own home where his attention was usually in high demand. He stepped outside and sat down on the front porch step. A moment later, the door opened, and his mother sat down beside him.

"Skip, that was the most exciting game I have ever seen. You did a wonderful job coaching those boys."

Skip turned to her in astonishment. "You saw it?"

"I wouldn't have missed it for anything in the world. Now that the girls are older, I'm able to attend your ballgames." Erin sat with him for a minute. "Well, I have to help Rose get lunch together." Quickly rising, she disappeared into the house.

His mother amazed him. She always seemed to know what he needed. Trailing her into the house, Skip trotted up the stairs to shower and change. It was late afternoon, and Skip was afraid that if he fell asleep now, he'd sleep for hours and then he'd lie awake half the night. So the refreshing shower helped wake him up.

Dressed in navy blue slacks and a striped shirt, Skip trotted down the stairs and joined the others in the living room. "We're eating in here? What about the girls?"

"We fed them and sent them outside to play," said Erin. "And since we're only having sandwiches, I thought we'd eat in here so Trevor has company. He needs to keep his leg propped. Now, would you ask the blessing?"

Skip bowed his head and thanked the Lord for the food. Then he grabbed a sandwich and dropped down in the recliner to eat it. The coffee table looked like a picnic lunch spread with a tray full of sandwiches, fresh fruit, a pitcher of iced tea, paper cups and plates, napkins, and plastic ware. And for a few minutes, the living room was quiet as the adults filled their plates and started to eat.

Rose looked at Skip. "I owe you a debt of gratitude for bringing my boys back to me." Turning to Erin, she continued. "Thanks for everything. I have really enjoyed getting to know you folks, and we're sure going to miss you when we go home."

"It's been our pleasure, Rose. You and the boys come visit us again. When are you leaving?"

"The boys and I will catch the Tuesday afternoon flight back to LA."

"Not me," said Robby. "I'm staying here. I like this town. I have a summer job lined up down at the pool, and I have already sent in an application for the community college. I should be hearing back from them soon."

"Erin?"

"Don't give it a second thought, Rose. He can stay with us. Skip always wanted a brother."

"All right. Then, I guess Trevor and I will be leaving on Tuesday morning."

Trevor cleared his throat and shook his head. "Mr. Cryder dropped the charges against me, and offered me my job back. I've already accepted. I don't plan to let him down again."

Rose looked from Robby to Trevor. "I hate the thought of going back to LA by myself."

"Then don't go," said Skip. "Stay in Forest Valley. We'd sure enjoy having you close by."

Rose sighed. "Skip, I don't know if I'm ready to come back to this little town. For years, I resented this town and your father's choice to stay here and be a law enforcement officer. Now, my own two sons would rather stay here than return to Los Angeles with me. And you played a big role in their decisions."

Skip caught his breath. That thought hadn't occurred to him. "I ... I'm sorry."

"Don't be. If it weren't for your influence, they'd probably be headed for jail."

"I didn't do anything."

Trevor's eyes widened and he looked around. "Then, who was that fellow that risked his life to save mine? It's lucky for me that it was dark out, because I can't imagine anyone in his right mind putting his life in such jeopardy to rescue a jerk who had just abandoned him a two-day walk from the nearest house."

"Skip, you did that?" gasped Rose. "That sounds just like Stephen. You look like him. You act like him. You talk like him. Would you like to come to LA with me?"

"Well, Robby, you just lost your position as Mom's favorite," said Trevor.

Robby grinned.

Skip cringed and broke eye contact. "Thanks for the invitation, Aunt Rose, but I can't. I have a family to take care of."

"I'll provide for them."

"No, that's all right. I like my job."

"We have a police department in Los Angeles. What do you say?"

Skip sighed. She was determined. Was this the kind of pressure she had exerted on his dad? Was she also going to harbor resentment against him for refusing?

"I'm sorry, Aunt Rose, but I love this town. I wouldn't be happy in a big city like Los Angeles." Seeing her moistened eyes, he grasped her hand. "Why don't you move back to Forest Valley? Then, we'd all be together."

"I think I will. I'm not making the same mistake twice. I appreciate everything you've done for my boys, Skip. Stephen couldn't possibly have done any better. He'd be awfully proud of you."

Your Eternity Awaits

Do You Know Jesus?

"For this is good and acceptable in the sight of God our Saviour;

Who will have all men to be saved, and to come unto the knowledge of the truth.

For there is one God, and one mediator between God and men, the man Christ Jesus."

I Timothy 2:3-5

Titus 2:11 says, **"For the grace of God that bringeth salvation hath appeared to all men."**

God is perfect, and He created mankind in His image.

Adam and Eve, the first man and woman, were created in perfection. They were perfect because God their Creator is perfect. And because of God's holiness, He cannot have fellowship with sinful people.

So when Adam and Eve sinned, all of God's creation immediately fell into a sinful state, and all babies were born with a sinful nature.

Romans 5:12 says, **"Wherefore, as by one man sin entered into the world, and death by sin; and so death passed upon all men, for that all have sinned."**

As a result, we were separated from our holy Creator.

Romans 3:23 says, **"For all have sinned, and come short of the glory of God."**

Then Romans 6:23 says, **"For the wages of sin is death …"**

Sin has a penalty – Death.

Everyone dies physically. That's the *first* death.

Revelation 20:14-15 says, **"And death and hell were cast into the lake of fire. This is the second death. And whosoever was not found written in the book of life was cast into the lake of fire."**

But God sent His Son to pay your penalty!

Romans 6:23 says, **"For the wages of sin is death; but the gift of God is eternal life through Jesus Christ our Lord."**

I Corinthians 15:3-4 says, **"For I delivered unto you first of all that which I also received, how that Christ died for our sins according to the scriptures; and that he was buried, and that he rose again the third day according to the scriptures."**

And God wishes none should perish. Not even you! So he made a way for you to escape eternal damnation in hell.

"For God so loved the world, that he gave his only begotten Son, that whosoever believeth in him should not perish, but have everlasting life." John 3:16

All You Have to do is Confess and Believe

Romans 10:9-10 says …

"That if thou shalt confess with thy mouth the Lord
Jesus, and shalt believe in thine heart that God hath raised
him from the dead, thou shalt be saved.

For with the heart man believeth unto righteousness; and
with the mouth, confession is made unto salvation."

Only those who accept Jesus as their Savior will have
their names written in the Lamb's Book of Life. It's not a
book of the names of every soul who's ever lived. No. It's
God's *Book of Eternal Life,* containing the names of
every soul who's trusted His Son as Savior.

But How Do I Get Saved?

1. Admit that you're a sinner and that you can't save
yourself.

2. Believe in the Lord Jesus Christ

3. Confess and repent of your sins.

"For whosoever shall call upon the name of the Lord shall
be saved." Romans 10:13

"And as it is appointed unto men once to die, but after this
the judgment." Hebrews 9:27

Preview of Book 5:

Skip Shaughnessy in A Score to Settle

When Cassandra's dad escapes prison, a double-crossing police officer helps him track down Skip. As a result, Skip finds himself trapped in impossible circumstances. He's dodging bullets and running from the police while carrying his five-year-old sister, with a sick partner in tow.

Other Books Written by Marjorie Strebe

Books in Skip's Action Series

Treasures in My Spiritual Hope Chest
Volumes 1 & 2

A King James devotional book with scripturally-sound lessons to help you grow spiritually when you read, understand, and apply God's Word to your life. You will discover priceless nuggets of God's truth in each devotional.

The Biography of a Child with Williams Syndrome
Third Edition

A special needs child with a mental handicap and developmental delays is falling through the cracks of every service designed to support her needs.

For more information, visit <u>www.marjiestrebe.com</u>, or email me at <u>kjvwriter@marjiestrebe.com</u>.